Truth [Vérité]

Book IV

by

Émile Zola

Truth [Vérité]

Book IV

by Émile Zola

ISBN: 978-93-68090-78-6

Published by

DOUBLE 9 BOOKS

2/13-B, Ansari Road
Daryaganj, New Delhi – 110002
info@double9books.com
www.double9books.com
Tel. 011-40042856

ABOUT THE AUTHOR

Émile Zola was a French novelist, journalist, and the most prominent figure in the literary school of naturalism. Zola is best known for his detailed and unflinching depictions of French society. His works explore themes of social injustice, human nature, and the influence of environment and heredity on personal fate.Zola's most famous work is the Les Rougon-Macquart series, a sprawling cycle of 20 novels that trace the lives of multiple generations of a family, set against the backdrop of Second Empire France. The series includes notable works like Germinal, a powerful novel about coal miners' struggles, Thérèse Raquin, a dark tale of passion and murder, and The Downfall (La Débâcle), which explores the impact of the Franco-Prussian War. His work was a critical reflection on the failings of society, and he championed the rights of the working class and the oppressed Zola's influence on literature was immense, and his works are considered foundational to the naturalist movement.

CONTENTS

CHAPTER I

When October arrived, Marc with joyous serenity repaired to Jonville, to take the modest post of village schoolmaster which he had formerly occupied there. Great quietude had now fallen on him, new courage and hope had followed the despair and weariness by which he had been prostrated after the monstrous trial of Rozan.

The whole of one's ideal is never realised, and Marc almost reproached himself for having relied on a splendid triumph. Human affairs do not progress by superb leaps and bounds, glorious *coups-de-théâtre*. It was chimerical to imagine that justice would be acclaimed by millions of lips, that the innocent prisoner would return amid a great national festival, transforming the country into a nation of brothers. All progress, the very slightest, the most legitimate, has been won by centuries of battling. Each forward step taken by mankind has demanded torrents of blood and tears, hecatombs of victims, sacrificing themselves for the good of future generations. Thus, in the eternal battle with the evil powers, it was unreasonable to expect a decisive victory, a supreme triumph, such as would fulfil all one's hopes, all one's dream of fraternity and equity among mankind.

Besides, Marc had ended by perceiving what a considerable step had been taken, after all, along that road of progress, which is so rough and deadly. While one is still in the thick of the fight, exposed to taunts and wounds, one does not always notice what ground one gains. One may even think oneself defeated when one has really made much progress and drawn very near to the goal. In this way, if the second condemnation of Simon had at first sight seemed a frightful defeat, it soon became apparent that the moral victory of his defenders was a great one. And there were all sorts of gains, a grouping of free minds and generous hearts, a broadening of human solidarity from one to the other end of the world, a sowing of truth and justice, which would end by sprouting up, even if the good grain should require many long winters to germinate in the furrows. And, again, it was only with the greatest difficulty that the reactionary castes, by dint of falsehoods and crimes, had for a time saved the rotten fabric of the past from utter collapse. It was none the less cracking on all sides; the blow dealt to it had rent it from top to bottom, and the blows of the future would complete its destruction and cast it down in a litter of wretched remnants.

Thus the only regret which Marc now experienced was that he had not been able to utilise that prodigious Simon affair as an admirable lesson of things which would have instructed the masses, enlightened them like a blaze of lightning. Never again, perhaps, would there be so complete and decisive a case. There was the complicity of all the powerful and all the oppressors banding themselves together to crush a poor innocent man, whose innocence imperilled the compact of human exploitation which the great ones of the world had signed together. There were all the averred crimes of the priests, soldiers, magistrates, and ministers, who, to continue deceiving the people, had piled the most extraordinary infamies one on another, and who had all been caught lying and assassinating, with no resource left them but to sink in an ocean of mud; and finally there had been the division of the country into two camps—on one hand the old authoritarian, antiquated, and condemned social order, on the other the young society of the future, free in mind already and ever tending towards increase of truth, equity, and peace. If Simon's innocence had been recognised, the reactionary past would have been struck down at one blow, and the joyous future would have appeared to the simplest, whose eyes, at last, would have been opened. Never before would the revolutionary axe have sunk so deeply into the old worm-eaten social edifice. Irresistible enthusiasm would have carried the nation towards the future city. In a few months the Simon affair would have done more for the emancipation of the masses and the reign of justice than a hundred years of ardent politics. And grief that things should have become so spoilt, and should have shattered the admirable work in their hands, was destined to abide in the hearts of the combatants as long as they might live.

But life continued, and it was necessary to fight again, fight on for ever. A step had been taken forward, and other steps remained to be taken. Duty demanded that, day by day, whatever the bitterness and often the obscurity of life, one should again give one's blood and one's tears, satisfied with gaining ground inch by inch, without even the reward of ever beholding the victory. Marc accepted that sacrifice, no longer hoping to see Simon's innocence recognised legally, definitively, and triumphantly by the whole people. He felt it was impossible to revive the affair amid the passions of the moment, for the innocent man's enemies would begin their atrocious campaign again, helped on by the cowardice of the multitude. It would be necessary, no doubt, to wait for the death of the personages involved in the case, for some transformation of parties, some new phase of politics, before the Government would be bold enough to apply once more to the Court of Cassation and ask it to efface that abominable page from the history of France.

Such seemed to be the conviction of even David and Simon, who, while leading a sequestered life, busy with their Pyrenean enterprise, watched for favourable incidents and circumstances, but felt that the situation tied their hands, and that it was necessary to remain waiting, unless indeed they wished to stir up another useless and dangerous onslaught.

Marc, being thus compelled to live in patience, reverted to his mission, to the one work on which he set his hopes—the instruction of the humble, the dissemination of truth by knowledge which alone could render a nation capable of equity. Great serenity had come to him, and he accepted the fact that generations of pupils would be necessary to rouse France from her numbness, deliver her from the poisons with which she had been gorged, and fill her with new blood which would transform her into the France of his old dreams—a generous, freedom-giving, and justice-dealing nation.

Never had Marc loved truth so passionately as he did now. In former times he had needed it, even as one needs the air one breathes; he had felt unable to live without it, sinking into intolerable anguish whenever it escaped him. At present, after seeing it attacked so furiously, denied, and hidden away in the depths of lies, like a corpse which would never revive, he believed in it still more; he felt that it was irresistible, possessed of sufficient power to blow up the world should men again try to bury it underground. It followed its road without ever taking an hour's rest; it marched on to its goal of light, and nothing would ever stop it. Marc shrugged his shoulders with ironical contempt when he beheld guilty men imagining that they had annihilated truth, that it lay beneath their feet as if it had ceased to exist. When the right moment came, truth would explode, scatter them like dust, and shine forth serenely and radiantly. And it was the certainty that truth, ever victorious, even after the lapse of ages, was upon his side, that lent Marc all necessary strength and composure to return to his work, and wait cheerfully for truth's triumph, even though it might only come after his own lifetime.

Moreover, the Simon case had imparted solidity to his convictions, breadth to his faith. He had previously passed condemnation on the *bourgeoisie,* which was exhausted by the abuse of its usurped power, which, from being a liberal class, had become a reactionary one, passing from free thought to the basest clericalism as it had felt the Church to be its natural ally in its career of rapine and enjoyment. And now he had seen the French *bourgeoisie* at work, he had seen it full of cowardice and falsehood, weak but tyrannical, denying all justice to the innocent, ready for every crime in order that it might not have to part with any of its millions, terrified as it was by the gradual awakening of the masses who claimed their due. And finding that *bourgeoisie* to be even more rotten, more stricken, than he had imagined, he held that it must promptly disappear if the nation did not desire to perish of incurable infection. Henceforth salvation was only to be found in the masses, in that new force—that inexhaustible reservoir of men, work, and energy. Marc felt that the masses were ever rising, like a new, rejuvenated race, bringing to social life more power for truth, justice, and happiness. And this confirmed him in the mission he had assumed, that seemingly modest mission of a village schoolmaster, which was in reality the apostolate of modern times, the only important work that could fashion the society of to-morrow. There was no loftier duty than that of striking down the errors and impostures of the Church and setting in their place truth as proclaimed by science, and human peace, based upon knowledge and solidarity. The France of the future was growing up in the rural districts, in the humblest, loneliest hamlets, and it was there that one must work and conquer.

Marc speedily set to work. He had to repair all the harm which Jauffre had caused by abandoning Jonville to Abbé Cognasse. But during the earlier days, while Marc and Geneviève were settling down, how delightful it was for them—reconciled as they were and renewing the love of youthful times—to find themselves again in the poor little nest of long ago! Sixteen years had passed, yet nothing seemed to be changed; the little school was just the same, with its tiny lodging and its strip of garden. The walls had merely been whitewashed, but the place seemed fairly clean, thanks to a good scouring which Geneviève superintended. She was never weary of summoning Marc to remind him of one thing and another, laughing happily at all that recalled the past.

'Oh! come and look at the picture of Useful Insects which you hung up in the classroom! It is still there.... I myself put up those pegs for the boys' hats.... In the cupboard yonder, you'll find the collection of solid bodies, which you cut out of beech wood.'

Marc hastened to her and joined in her laughter. And in his turn he summoned her to him: 'Come upstairs—make haste! Do you see that date cut with a knife in the wall of the alcove? Don't you remember that I did that the day Louise was born?... And just recollect, when we were in bed, we used to look at that crack in the ceiling, and jest about it, saying that the stars were watching and smiling at us.'

Then, as they went through the little garden, they burst into exclamations: 'Why, look at the old fig tree! It hasn't changed a bit; we might have left it only yesterday.... Ah! we had a border of strawberries in the place of that sorrel; we shall have to plant one again.... The pump has been changed—that's a blessing! Perhaps we shall be able to get water with this one.... Why, there's our seat, our seat under the creeper! We must sit down and kiss each other—all the young kisses of long ago in a good kiss of to-day.'

They felt moved to tears, and for an instant they lingered embracing, amid that delightful renewal of their happiness. Great courage came to them from the sight of those friendly surroundings, where they had never shed a tear. Everything they saw drew them more closely together, and seemed to promise them victory.

With respect to their daughter Louise, a separation had become necessary at the very outset. She had been obliged to leave them for the Training School of Fontenay, to which she had secured admission. Her tastes and her love for her father had made her desirous of becoming a mere schoolmistress, even as he was a mere village schoolmaster. And Marc and Geneviève, remaining alone with little Clément, saddened by their daughter's departure, though they knew it to be necessary, drew yet closer together, in order to deaden their sense of that sudden void. True, Clément remained with them, and gave them occupation. He was now becoming quite a little man, and it was with affectionate solicitude that they watched over the awakening of his faculties.

Besides, Marc prevailed on Geneviève to undertake the management of the adjoining girls' school—that is after requesting Salvan to intervene with Le Barazer with a view to her appointment to the post. It will be remembered that immediately after her convent days she had obtained the necessary certificates, and that if she had not taken charge of the girls' school when her husband was first appointed to Jonville, it had been because Mademoiselle Mazeline had then held the post. But the advancement now given to Jauffre and his wife had left both posts vacant, and it seemed best that the two schools should be confided to Marc and Geneviève, the husband taking the boys and the wife the girls—this indeed being an arrangement which the authorities always preferred.

Marc, for his part, perceived all sorts of advantages in it: the teaching would proceed on the same lines in both schools; he would have a devoted collaborator who would help instead of trying to thwart him in his advance towards the future. And, again, though Geneviève had given him no cause for anxiety since her return, she would find occupation for her mind; she would be compelled to recover and exert her reason in acting as a teacher, a guardian of the little maids who would be the wives and mothers of to-morrow. Besides, would not their union be perfected? would they not be blended for ever, if, with all faith and all affection, they should share the same blessed work of teaching the poor and lowly, from whom the felicity of the future would spring? When a notification of the appointment arrived, fresh joy came to them; it was as if they now had but one heart and one brain.

But in what a ruinous and uneasy state did Marc now find that village of Jonville which he had loved so well! He remembered his first struggles with the terrible Abbé Cognasse, and how he had triumphed by securing the support of Mayor Martineau, that well-to-do, illiterate but sensible peasant, who retained all a peasant's racial antipathy for the priests—those lazy fellows, who lived well and did nothing. Between them, Marc and Martineau had begun to secularise the parish; the schoolmaster no longer sang in the choir, no longer rang the bell for Mass, no longer conducted his pupils to the Catechism classes; while the Mayor and the parish council escaped from routine and favoured the evolution which gave the school precedence over the Church. Thanks to the action Marc brought to bear on his boys and their parents, and the influence he exercised at the parish offices, where he held the post of secretary, he had seen great prosperity set in around him. But as soon as he had been transferred to Maillebois, Martineau, falling into the hands of Jauffre, the man of the Congregations, had speedily weakened. Indeed, he was incapable of action when he did not feel himself supported by a resolute will. Racial prudence deterred him from expressing an opinion of his own; he sided with the priest or with the schoolmaster according as one or the other proved to be the stronger. Thus, while Jauffre, thinking merely of his own advancement, chanted the litanies, rang the bell, and attended the Communion, Abbé Cognasse gradually became master of the parish, setting the Mayor and the council beneath his heel, to the secret delight of the beautiful Madame Martineau, who, though not piously inclined, was very fond of displaying new gowns at High Mass on days of festival. Never had there been a plainer demonstration of the axiom, 'According to the worth of the schoolmaster, such is the worth of the school; and according to the worth of the school, such is the worth of the parish.' In very few years, indeed, the prosperity which had declared itself in Jonville, the ground which had been gained, thanks to Marc, was lost. The village retrograded, its life died away in increasing torpor after Jauffre had delivered Martineau and his fellow-parishioners into the hands of the triumphant Cognasse.

In this way sixteen years elapsed, bringing disaster. All moral and intellectual decline leads inevitably to material misery. There is no country where the Roman Church has reigned as absolute sovereign that is not now a dead country. Ignorance, error, and base credulity render men powerless. And what can be the use of exercising one's will, acting and progressing, if one be a mere toy in the hands of a Deity who plays with one according to his fancy? That Deity suffices, supplies the place of everything. At the end of such a religion of terrestrial and human nothingness, there is but stupidity, inertia, surrender into the hands of Providence, mere routine in the avocations of life, idleness, and want. Jauffre let his boys gorge themselves with Bible history and Catechism, while in their peasant families all ideas of any improved system of cultivating the land were regarded with increasing suspicion. They knew nothing of those matters, they would not learn. Fields remained unproductive, crops were lost for want of intelligent care. Then effort seemed excessive and useless, and the countryside became impoverished, deserted, though above it there still shone the all-powerful and fructifying sun—that ignored, insulted god of life.

The decline of Jonville had become yet more marked after Abbé Cognasse had prevailed on the weak Martineau to allow the parish to be dedicated to the Sacred Heart in a pompous and well-remembered ceremony. The peasants were still waiting for that Sacred Heart to bring them the wondrous promised harvests by dispelling the hailstorms and granting rain and fine weather in due season. By way of result one only found more imbecility weighing on the parish, a sleepy waiting for divine intervention, the slow agony of fanatical believers, in whom all power of initiative has been destroyed, and who, if their Deity did not nourish them, would let themselves starve rather than raise an arm.

During the first days that followed his return, Marc, on taking a few country walks with Geneviève, felt quite distressed by all the incompetency and neglect he beheld. The fields were ill-kept, the roads scarcely passable. One morning they went as far as Le Moreux, where they found Mignot installing himself in his wretched school, and feeling as grieved as they were that the district should have fallen into such a deplorable state.

'You have no idea, my friends,' said he, 'of the ravages of that terrible Cognasse. He exercises some little restraint at Jonville; but here, in this lonely village, whose inhabitants are too miserly to pay for a priest of their own, he terrorises and sabres everybody. Of late years, he and his creature Chagnat, while reigning here, virtually suppressed the Mayor, Saleur, who felt flattered at being re-elected every time, but who turned all the worries of his office over to his secretary, Chagnat, and by way of exhibiting his person, let himself be taken to Mass, though at heart he scarcely cared for the priests.... Ah! how well I now understand the torments of poor Férou, his exasperation, and the fit of lunacy which led to his martyrdom.'

With a quivering gesture Marc indicated that he was haunted by the thought of that unhappy man, struck down by a revolver-shot yonder, under the burning sun. 'When I came in just now, he seemed to rise before me. Famished, having only his scanty pay to provide for himself, his wife, and his children, he endured untold agony at feeling that he was the only intelligent, the only educated, man among all those ignorant dolts living at their ease, who disdained him for his poverty and feared him for his attainments, which humiliated them.... That explains, too, the power acquired by Chagnat over the Mayor, the latter's one desire being to live in peace on his income, in the somnolent state of a man whose appetite is satisfied.'

'But the whole parish is like that,' Mignot replied. 'There are no poor, and each peasant remains content with what he harvests, not in a spirit of wisdom, but from a kind of egotism, ignorance, and laziness. If they are perpetually quarrelling with the priest, it is because they accuse him of slighting them, of not giving them the Masses and other ceremonies to which they consider themselves entitled. Thanks to Chagnat, in his time something like an understanding was arrived at, and, indeed, all that was said and done here in honour of St. Antony of Padua can hardly be pictured.... But the result of Chagnat's *régime* is deplorable; I found the school as dirty as a cowshed; one might have thought that the Chagnats had lodged all the cattle of the district in it, and I had to engage a woman to help me to scour and scrape everything.'

Geneviève, meantime, had become dreamy; her glance seemed to wander away to far-off memories. 'Ah! poor Férou!' she murmured, 'I was not always kind to him and his family. That is one of my regrets. But how can one remedy so much suffering and disaster? We have so little power, we are still so few. There are times when I despair.' Then, suddenly waking up, as it were, and smiling, she nestled close to her husband and resumed: 'There, there, don't scold me, my dear, I did wrong to speak like that. But you must allow me enough time to become fearless and reproachless as you yourself are.... Come, it's understood, we are going to set to work, and we shall conquer.'

Thereupon they all became merry, and Mignot, who wished to escort his friends a little way, ended by accompanying them almost to Jonville. There, at the roadside, stood a large square building, a kind of factory, the branch establishment of the Good Shepherd of Beaumont, which had been promised at the time of the consecration of the parish to the Sacred Heart, and which had now been working for several years. The fine clerical folk had made a great noise about the prosperity which such an establishment would bring with it: all the daughters of the peasants would find employment and become skilful workwomen, there would be a great improvement in their morality, drones and gadabouts would be duly corrected, and the business might end by endowing the district with quite an industry.

The specialty of the Good Shepherd establishments was to provide the big drapery shops of Paris with petticoats, knickers, and chemises—the finest, most ornamental, and most delicate feminine body linen. At Jonville, under the superintendence of some ten sisters, two hundred girls worked from morning till night, trying their eyes over all that rich and fashionable underwear, which was often destined for strange festivities. And those two hundred little *lingères* constituted but a tiny fraction of all the poor hirelings who were thus exploited, for the Order had establishments from one to the other end of France; nearly fifty thousand girls toiled in its workshops, scantily paid, ill-treated, and ill-fed, while they earned for it millions of francs. At Jonville, there had been speedy disenchantment, none of the fine promises had been fulfilled, the establishment seemed a gulf which swallowed up the last energies of the region. The farms were raided and their women folk carried off, the peasants could no longer keep their daughters with them,—the girls all dreamt of becoming young ladies, of spending their days on chairs, engaged in light work. But they soon repented of their folly, for what with the long hours of enforced immobility, the exhausting strain of unremitting application, never was there more frightful drudgery; the stomach remained empty, the head became heavy, there was no time for sleep in summer, and there was no fire in winter. The place was a prison-house, where, under the pretext of practising charity, of promoting morality, woman was exploited in the most frightful manner, sweated in her flesh, stupefied in her intelligence, turned into a beast of burden, from whom the greatest gain possible was extracted. And scandals burst forth at Jonville; one girl nearly perished of cold and starvation, another became half mad, while another, turned out of doors penniless after years of crushing toil, rebelled, and threatened the good sisters with a sensational lawsuit. [1]

> [1] In the above account of the Good Shepherd establishments, M. Zola has made use of numerous incidents brought to light by proceedings in the French law courts, and also by the action of the Bishop of Nancy, who, in attempting to put a stop to abominable practices, incurred the odium of all the money-grubbing Congregations.—*Trans.*

Marc, stopping short on the road, looked at the big factory, silent like a prison, deathly like a cloister, where so many young lives were wearing themselves away, nothing carolling, meanwhile, the happiness of fruitful work.

'One source of the Church's strength,' said he, 'a very simple matter in practice, is that she stoops to present-day requirements and borrows our own weapons to fight us. She manufactures and she trades; there is no object or article of daily consumption that she does not produce or sell, from clothes to *liqueurs*. Several Orders are merely industrial associations, which undersell other people, as they secure labour for next to nothing, and thus compete disloyally with our smaller producers. The millions of francs they gain go into the cash-boxes of the Black Band, supplying sinews for the war of extermination which is waged against us, swelling the thousands of millions which the Congregations possess already, and which may render them so redoubtable.'

Geneviève and Mignot had listened thoughtfully. And a moment of anxious silence now followed amid the evening quietude, while the sunset cast a great pink glow on the closed and mournful factory of the Good Shepherd.

'Why, I myself seem to be despairing now!' Marc resumed gaily. 'They are still very powerful, it is certain. But we have a book on our side, the little book of elementary knowledge, which brings truth with it, and which will end by for ever overcoming the falsehoods they have circulated for so many centuries. All our strength is in that, Mignot. They may accumulate ruins here, they may lead poor ignorant folk backward, and destroy the little good done by us formerly; but it will suffice for us to resume our efforts to bring about progress by knowledge, and we shall regain the lost ground, and continue to advance until we at last reach the City of solidarity and peace. Their prison-house of the Good Shepherd will crumble like all others, their Sacred Heart will go whither all the gross fetiches of the dead religions have gone. You hear me, Mignot; each pupil in whom you instil a little truth will be another helper in the cause of justice. So to work, to work! Victory is certain, whatever difficulties and sufferings may be encountered on the road!'

That cry of faith and everlasting hope rang out across the quiet countryside amid the calm setting of the planet which foretold a bright to-morrow. And Mignot bravely returned to his task at Le Moreux, while Marc and Geneviève went homeward to begin their work at Jonville.

Arduous work it was, requiring much will and patience, for it was necessary to free Mayor Martineau, the parish council, and indeed the whole village from the hands of the priest, who was determined not to relax his hold. On hearing of Marc's appointment, Abbé Cognasse, instead of evincing any anger or fear of the redoubtable adversary who was being sent to face him, had contented himself with shrugging his shoulders and affecting extreme contempt. He said on all sides that this beaten man, this disgraced mediocrity, who had lost all honour by his complicity in the Simon case, would not remain six months at Jonville. His superiors had merely sent him there in order to finish him off, not wishing to execute him at one blow. In reality, no doubt, Abbé Cognasse scarcely felt at ease, for he knew the man he had to deal with—a man all calmness and strength, derived from his reliance on truth. And that the priest plainly scented danger was shown by the prudence and *sangfroid* which he himself strove to preserve, for fear of spoiling everything if he should yield to some of his customary fits of passion. Thus the unexpected spectacle of a superbly diplomatic Abbé Cognasse, who left to Providence the duty of striking down the enemy, was presented to the village. As his servant Palmyre, who with increasing age had become quite terrible, did not possess sufficient self-restraint to imitate his silent contempt, he scolded her in public when she ventured to declare that the new schoolmaster had stolen some consecrated wafers from the church at Maillebois for the purpose of profaning them in the presence of his pupils. That was not proved, said the Abbé, nor was there any proof of the story that hell had lent Marc a devil, who, on being summoned, stepped out of the wall and helped him with his class-work. Indoors, however, all was agreement between the priest and the servant, who both displayed extraordinary greed and avarice, the former picking up as many Masses as possible, the latter keeping the accounts, and growling angrily when money did not come in. With reference to Marc, then, there ensued, on the Abbé's part, a stealthy and venomous campaign, with the object of destroying both the master and his school, in order that he, Cognasse, might continue to reign over the parish.

Marc, on his side, behaved as if the Church and the priest did not exist. To win back Martineau, the council, and the inhabitants, he contented himself with teaching the truth, with promoting the triumph of reason over ridiculous dogmas, limiting himself strictly to his duties as a master, convinced as he was that the true and the good would prove victorious when he should have fashioned hearts and minds capable of will and understanding. He had necessarily resumed the duties of secretary at the parish office, but he there contented himself with discreetly advising Martineau, who at heart was well pleased by his return. The Mayor had already had a quarrel with his wife respecting the chanting of Mass, which chanting Abbé Cognasse had done away with now that Jauffre was no longer there. And there was also the ancient and everlasting quarrel about the church clock, which would not work. The first thing which showed that a change had taken place at Jonville was the vote of a sum of three hundred francs by the council for the purchase of a new clock which was fixed to the pediment of the parish offices. This seemed a very bold step to take, but it met with the approval of the villagers. They would at last know the correct time, which the rusty, old, worn-out clock of the church no longer gave. However, Marc avoided any semblance of triumph; he knew that years would be needed to regain all the lost ground. Each day would bring a little progress, and he patiently sowed the future, convinced that those peasants would come over to his side when they found in truth the one sole source of health, prosperity, and peace.

And now, for Marc and Geneviève, came fruitful years of work and happiness. He, in particular, had never felt so courageous and strong. The loving return of his wife, and the complete union which had followed it, brought him fresh power, for his life now accorded with his work. In former times he had greatly suffered at finding that, while he claimed to teach truth to others, he could not convince the companion of his life, the wife he loved, the mother of his children; and he had felt hampered in his task of wresting others from error when, from weakness or powerlessness, he tolerated error in his own home. But now he possessed irresistible strength, all the authority which comes to one from example, from the realisation of happiness at the family hearth through perfect agreement and a common faith. And what healthy delight there was in the prosecution of the same work by the husband and the wife, acting in conjunction one with the other, and yet freely, each retaining the exercise of his or her individuality! Moments of weakness still came occasionally to Geneviève, but Marc scarcely intervened; he preferred to let her regret and repair the errors arising from the past, of her own accord.

Every evening, when the boys and girls had gone home, the master and the mistress found themselves together in their little lodging, and talked of the children confided to them, taking account of the day's work, and coming to an understanding respecting the work of the morrow, though without binding themselves to identical programmes. Geneviève, being sentimentally inclined, endeavoured the more particularly to make sincere and happy creatures of her girls, trying to free them from the ancient slavery less by knowledge than by sense and love, for fear of casting them into pride and solitude. Marc, perhaps, would have gone further, and have fed both boys and girls on the same knowledge, leaving life to indicate the social *rôle* of each sex. Before long the great regret experienced by himself and his wife was that they did not direct a mixed school, like Mignot's at Le Moreux, whose population of little more than two hundred souls supplied scarcely a dozen boys and as many girls. At Jonville, which numbered nearly eight hundred inhabitants, the master had some thirty boys under him, and the mistress some thirty girls. Had they been united, what a fine class there would have been—Marc acting as director, and Geneviève as his assistant! Such indeed was their idea; had they been in authority they would no longer have separated the girls from the boys; they would have entrusted all those little folk to a married couple, a father and a mother, who would have educated and reared them one with the other as if they all belonged to their own family. They held that all sorts of advantages would result from such a course, a more logical apprenticeship of life, excellent emulation, more frank and gentle manners. In particular, the adjunction of the wife to the husband as an assistant seemed likely to prove fruitful in good results. Briefly, they would have liked to pull down the wall which separated their pupils from one another, in such wise as to have had but one school, a little miniature world in which he would have set his virility, she her tenderness, and what good work would they not then have accomplished, devoting themselves entirely to those little couples of the future!

But the regulations had to be observed, and Marc, on resuming his work, pursued the methods that he had followed at Maillebois for fifteen years. His class was smaller than it had been there, and his resources were more limited; but he had the satisfaction of being almost *en famille*, and his action became more direct and efficacious. After all, what did it matter if the number of pupils whom he fashioned into men was only a score or so? Had each schoolmaster in all the little villages followed Marc's example, so as to endow the nation with twenty just and sensible men, the result would have sufficed to make France the emancipator of the world. Another source of contentment for Marc was that he secured almost complete liberty of action from Mauraisin's successor, the new Elementary Inspector, M. Mauroy, to whom Le Barazer, whose friend he was, had discreetly given special instructions. The village was so small that Marc's doings could not attract much attention, and thus he was able to pursue his methods without any great interference. As a first step, he again got rid of all religious emblems, all pictures, copybooks, and books in which the supernatural was shown triumphant, and in which war, massacre, and rapine appeared as ideals of power and beauty. He considered that it was a crime to poison a lad's brain with a belief in miracles, and to set brute force, assassination, and theft in the front rank as manly and patriotic duties. Such teaching could only produce imbecile inertia, sudden criminal frenzy, iniquity, and wretchedness. Marc's dream, on the contrary, was to set pictures of work and peace before his pupils, to show sovereign reason ruling the world, justice establishing brotherliness among men, the ancient violence of warlike ages being condemned, and giving place to agreement among all nations, in order that they might arrive at the greatest possible happiness. And having rid his class of the poisonous ferments of the past, Marc particularly instructed his pupils in civic morality, striving to make each a citizen well informed about his country, and able to serve and love it, without setting it apart from the rest of mankind. Marc held that France ought no longer to dream of conquering the world by arms, but rather by the irresistible force of ideas, and by setting an example of so much freedom, truth, and equity, that she would deliver all other countries and enjoy the glory of founding with them the great confederation of free and brotherly nations.

For the rest, Marc tried to conform to the school programmes, though, as they were very heavy, he occasionally set them aside. Experience had taught him that learning was nothing if one did not understand what one learnt and if one could not put it to use. Accordingly, without excluding books, he gave great development to oral lessons, and, once again, he strove to rejuvenate himself, to share the pastimes of his pupils, and descend, as it were, to their mental level, in such wise that, like them, he seemed to be learning, seeking truth, and making discoveries. It was in the fields also that he explained to them how the soil ought to be cultivated, and he took them to carpenters, locksmiths, and masons in order that they might acquire correct ideas of manual work. In his opinion, moreover, it was fit that gymnastics should partake of the character of amusement, and thus playtime was largely devoted to bodily exercise. Again, Marc took on himself the office of a judge; he requested his boys to lay all their little differences before him, and he strove to make his decisions acceptable to all parties; for not only did he possess absolute faith in the beneficent power of truth upon young minds, but he was also convinced of the necessity of equity to content and ripen them. By truth and justice towards love: such was his motto. A boy to whom one never tells a falsehood, whom one treats invariably with justice, becomes a friendly, sensible, intelligent, and healthy man. And this was why Marc kept such a careful watch over the books which the curriculum compelled him to place in the hands of his pupils; for he well knew that the best of them, written with the most excellent intentions, were still full of ancient falsehoods, the great iniquities consecrated by history. If he distrusted phrases and words, the sense of which seemed likely to escape his little peasants, and endeavoured to interpret them in clear and simple language, he feared yet more the dangerous legends, the errors of articles of faith, the abominable notions set forth in the name of a mendacious religion and a false patriotism. There was often no difference between the books written by clerics for the Brothers' schools and those which university men prepared for the secular ones. The intentional errors contained in the former were reproduced in the latter, and it was impossible for Marc to refrain from intervening and refuting those errors by verbal explanations, since it was essentially his task to fight the Congregational system of teaching, that source of all falsehood and all misery.

For four years Marc and Geneviève worked on, modestly but efficaciously, silently accomplishing as much good as was possible in their little sphere. Generations of children followed one another; and to the master and the mistress it seemed that fifty years would have sufficed to rejuvenate the world, if each child, on reaching maturity, had contributed to it a little more truth and justice. Four years of effort had certainly not yielded a marked result, but many good symptoms were manifest; the future was already rising from the fruitful soil, sown so perseveringly.

Salvan, after being pensioned off, had ended by taking up his abode at Jonville, in a little house left him by a cousin. He lived there like a sage, with just enough money to provide for his wants and indulge in the cultivation of a few flowers. In his garden, under an arbour of roses and clematis, there was a large stone table, round which on Sundays he liked to assemble a few friends, former pupils of the Training College, who chatted, fraternised, and indulged together in fine dreams. Salvan was the patriarch of the gathering, which Marc joined every Sunday, his satisfaction being complete whenever he there met Joulic, his successor at Maillebois, from whom he obtained information about his old school. Joulic was a tall, slim, fair young man, gentle yet energetic, who had taken to the teaching profession by taste, and in order to escape the brutifying office life from which his father, a petty clerk, had suffered. One of Salvan's best pupils, he brought to his work a mind liberated from all absurd dogmas, won over entirely to experimental methods. And thanks to a great deal of shrewdness and quiet firmness, which had enabled him to avoid the traps set for him by the Congregations, he proved very successful at Maillebois. He had lately married a schoolmaster's daughter, a fair little creature, gentle like himself, and this had helped to make his school an abode of gaiety and peace.

One Sunday, when Marc reached Salvan's, he found Joulic already chatting with the master of the house at the stone table in the flowery arbour, and they, at the sight of him, at once made merry.

'Come on, my friend!' cried Salvan; 'here's Joulic telling me that some more boys have left the Brothers' school at Maillebois. People say that we are beaten, but we work on quietly, and our action spreads and triumphs more and more each year!'

'Yes,' Joulic added, 'everything is progressing at Maillebois, which once seemed to be the rotten borough of clericalism.... Brother Joachim, Fulgence's successor, is certainly a very clever man, as artful and as prudent as the other was wild and rough, but he cannot overcome the distrust of the families of the town—the turn which public opinion has taken against the Congregational schools, where the studies are indifferent and the morals doubtful. Simon may have been reconvicted, but, all the same, the ghost of Gorgias returns to the spot which he polluted, and his very defenders are haunted by the memory of his crime. And thus I recruit each boy who leaves the Ignorantines.'

Marc, who had now seated himself, laughed and thanked his young colleague. 'You don't know how much your news pleases me, my dear Joulic,' he replied. 'When I quitted Maillebois I left a part of my heart there, and I felt worried as to what might become of the work which I had been pursuing for fifteen years; but I have long ceased to feel any anxiety, knowing my old school to be in such capable hands as yours. Yes, if some of the poison which infected Maillebois has been eliminated, it is because the pupils who quit you, year by year, become men of sense and equity.... Ask your old master, Salvan, what he thinks of you.'

But Joulic with a gesture curtailed Marc's praises. 'No, no,' said he, 'I am only a pawn in the great battle. If I am worth anything I owe it to my training, so that the chief merit belongs to our master. Besides, I am not alone at Maillebois; I derive the most precious help, I will even say the greatest support, from Mademoiselle Mazeline. She has often consoled and encouraged me. You cannot imagine how much moral energy that gentle and sensible woman possesses. A large part of our success is due to her, for it is she who has gradually won family people over to our cause by turning out so many good wives and mothers.... When a woman personifies truth, justice, and love, she becomes the greatest power in the world——'

Joulic paused, for at that moment Mignot made his appearance. Those Sunday meetings brought delightful relaxation to Marc's former assistant, who cheerfully walked the two and a half miles which separated Le Moreux from Jonville. Having caught Joulic's last words, he at once exclaimed: 'Ah! Mademoiselle Mazeline—do you know that I wanted to marry her? I never mentioned it, but I may admit it now.... It is all very well to say that she is plain; but at Maillebois, on seeing how good and sensible, how admirable she was, I dreamt of her. And one day I told her of my idea. You should have seen how moved she was—grave, yet smiling, quite sisterly! She explained her position to me, saying that she was too old—already five and thirty, just my own age. Besides, she added, her girls had become her family, and she had long renounced all idea of living for herself.... Yet I fancy that my proposal stirred up some old regrets.... Briefly, we continued good friends, and I decided to remain a bachelor, though this occasionally embarrasses me at Le Moreux, on account of my girl pupils, who would be better cared for by a woman.'

Then he, also, gave some good news of the state of feeling in his parish. All the crass ignorance and error, which Chagnat had voluntarily allowed to accumulate there, were beginning to disappear. Saleur, the Mayor, had experienced great trouble with his son, Honoré, whom he had sent to the Lycée of Beaumont, where he had been stuffed by the chaplain with as much religious knowledge as he would have acquired in a seminary—in such wise that, after being appointed to the management of a little Catholic bank in Paris, he had come to grief there by practices which had nearly landed him in a criminal court. Since then his father, the ex-grazier, who at heart had never liked the priests, never wearied of denouncing what he called the Black Band, exasperated as he was by the downfall of his son, which had quite upset his comfortable life as an enriched peasant. And thus, at each fresh quarrel with Abbé Cognasse, he sided with schoolmaster Mignot, carrying the parish council with him, and threatening to have nothing more to do with the Church if the priest should still treat the inhabitants as a subjugated flock. Indeed, never before had that lonely sluggish village of Le Moreux so freely granted admittance to the new ideas. In part this was due to the better position which the schoolmasters had secured of recent years. Various laws had been passed improving their circumstances, and the lowest annual salaries were now fixed at twelve hundred francs without any deductions. [2] It had not been necessary to wait long for the result of this change. If Férou, ill-paid, ragged, and wretched, had formerly incurred the contempt of the peasantry on being compared by them with Abbé Cognasse, who waxed fat on surplice-fees and presents, and was therefore honoured and feared, Mignot, on the contrary, being able to live in a dignified way, had risen to his proper position—that is the first. Indeed, in that century-old struggle between the Church and the school, the whole region was now favouring the latter, whose victory appeared to be certain.

[2] It is true that such laws have been passed, but in various respects they are merely of a permissive character, and the financial circumstances of the French Government have hitherto prevented the realisation of provisions favoured by the Legislature. Several publications issued in the autumn of 1902, since M. Zola's death, have shown this to be the case. M. Zola, however, in this last section of 'Truth,' anticipates rather than follows events, as will plainly appear in the final chapters; and, as a strong movement in favour of the secular schoolmasters is now following the suppression of the Congregational schools, considerable improvement in the former's position will probably take place before long.—*Trans.*

'My peasants are still very ignorant,' Mignot continued. 'You cannot imagine what a sluggish spot Le Moreux is, all numbness and routine. The peasants have lands of their own, they have never lacked bread, and they would submit to be fleeced as in former times rather than turn to anything novel and strange.... But there is some change all the same; I can see it by the way they take off their hats to me, and the more and more preponderating position which the school assumes in their estimation. And, by the way, this morning, when Abbé Cognasse came over to say Mass, there were just three women and a boy in the church. When the Abbé went off he banged the vestry door behind him, threatening that he wouldn't come back any more, as it was useless for him to walk all that distance for nobody.'

Marc began to laugh. 'Yes,' said he, 'I've heard that the Abbé is getting surly again at Le Moreux. Here he still restrains himself, and strives to win the battle by diplomatic artfulness, particularly with the women, for his superiors have taught him, no doubt, that one is never beaten so long as one has the women on one's side. I have been told that he frequently goes to Valmarie to see Father Crabot, and it is surely there that he acquires that unctuous, caressing way with the ladies which surprises one so much in a rough, brutal man of his stamp. When he again loses his temper, as he will some day, it will be all over.... Besides, things are quite satisfactory at Jonville. We gain a little ground every year; the parish is regaining prosperity and health. In consequence of the recent scandals the peasants no longer allow their daughters to work at the factory of the Good Shepherd. And it seems that the parish council—Martineau at the head of it—greatly regrets its imbecility in having allowed Abbé Cognasse and Jauffre to dedicate Jonville to the Sacred Heart. I am on the lookout for an opportunity to efface that remembrance, and I shall end by finding one.'

There came a short pause. Then Salvan, who had listened complacently, said, by way of conclusion, in his quiet, cheerful manner: 'All that is very encouraging. Maillebois, Jonville, and Le Moreux are advancing towards those better times for which we have battled. The others thought they would conquer us, exterminate us for ever, and indeed, for months, it seemed as if we were dead; but now comes the slow awakening, the seed has germinated in the ground; it was sufficient for us to resume our work in silence, and the good grain grows and flowers once more. And now nothing will hinder the future harvest. The fact is that we have been on the side of truth, which nothing can destroy, nothing arrest in its splendour.... No doubt, things are not quite satisfactory at Beaumont. The sons of Doutrequin, that old Republican of the heroic times who lapsed into clericalism, have obtained advancement, and Mademoiselle Rouzaire still gorges her girls with Bible history and Catechism. But even public feeling at Beaumont is beginning to change. Moreover, Mauraisin has not succeeded at the Training College. Some of the students have told me jocularly that my ghost appears to him there, and paralyses him with fear. The fact is that the impulse had been given, and he has found it impossible to stop the emancipation of the schoolmaster. I even hope that we shall soon be rid of him.... And a very hopeful symptom is that, behind Maillebois, Jonville, and Le Moreux, there are other small towns and villages, nearly all in fact, where the schoolmaster is defeating the priest, and setting the secular school erect on the ruins of the Congregational school. Reason is triumphing, and justice and truth are slowly increasing their sphere of conquest at Dherbecourt, Juilleroy, Rouville, and Les Bordes. It is a general awakening, an irresistible movement, carrying France towards her liberating mission.'

'But it is your work!' cried Marc with sudden enthusiasm. 'There is a pupil of yours in each of the localities you have named. They are the children of your heart and mind; it was you who sent them as missionaries into lonely country districts to diffuse the new gospel of truth and justice. If people are at last awaking, returning to manly dignity, becoming an equitable, free, and healthy democracy, it is because a generation of your pupils is now installed in our classrooms, instructing the young, and making true citizens of them. You are the good workman; you realised that no progress is possible save by reason and knowledge.'

Then Joulic and Mignot seconded Marc with similar enthusiasm: 'Yes, yes, you have been the father, we are your children! The country will only be worth what the schoolmasters may make it, and the schoolmasters themselves can only be worth what the training colleges have made them.'

Salvan, who seemed very moved, protested with modest *bonhomie*. 'Men like me, my friends? Why, there are some everywhere; there will be plenty when they are allowed to act. Le Barazer helped me a great deal by keeping me at my post, and not tying me down too much. What I did? Why, Mauraisin himself is almost obliged to do the same, for the evolution carries him on; the work, once begun, never stops. And you'll see, Mauraisin's successor will turn out even better masters than those who passed through my hands.... One thing which delights me, and which you have not mentioned, is that nowadays students are recruited much more easily for the training colleges. What made me most anxious in former times was the distrust, the contempt into which the teaching profession had fallen, ill-paid, unhonoured as it was. But since the salaries have been increased, now that real honour attaches to the humblest members of the profession, candidates arrive from all quarters, so that one is able to pick and choose, and form an excellent staff.... And if I have rendered any services you may be sure that, on seeing my work continued and fulfilled, I feel rewarded beyond all my hopes. At present I desire to remain a mere spectator of things; I applaud your efforts, and live happily in my little garden, delighted to be forgotten by everybody—excepting you, my lads.'

He ceased speaking, and a thrill of feeling passed through the others as they sat there at the large stone table in the arbour, balmy with the perfume of the roses, while from the verdant garden, from the whole stretch of country around them, infinite serenity was wafted.

Every year since her parents had removed to Jonville, Louise had spent the vacation with them. Her brother Clément would now soon be ten years old, and Marc still kept him in his school, giving him that elementary education which he would have liked to have seen generalised, applied to all the children of the nation to whatever class they might belong, in order that one might have based upon it, in accordance with the tastes and talents of the pupils, a system of general and gratuitous secondary education. If his own tastes should be shared by his son, he intended to prepare him for the Training College of Beaumont, for the great national work of salvation would lie in the humble village schools for many years longer. Louise also had disinterestedly set her ambition upon becoming an elementary teacher. And, indeed, on quitting the school of Fontenay with the necessary certificates, she was, to her great delight, appointed assistant to her former and well-loved mistress, Mademoiselle Mazeline, at Maillebois.

At that time Louise was nineteen years of age. Salvan had intervened with Le Barazer to secure her appointment, which passed virtually unnoticed. The times were changing more and more; the period of delirium—when the mere names of Simon and Froment had sufficed to raise a tempest—was quite over. And this emboldened Le Barazer, six months later, to appoint Simon's son Joseph as assistant to Joulic. Joseph, it should be said, had made his *début* at Dherbecourt after quitting the Training College two years previously with an excellent record. As advancement his transfer to Maillebois was of little account, but it was a somewhat bold action to place him in a school where his presence implied at least some preliminary rehabilitation of his father. For a moment there was a slight outcry, the Congregations tried to stir up the parents of the town; but the new assistant soon won their favour, for he behaved very discreetly, gently, yet firmly, in all his intercourse with the children.

One incident which at that time plainly indicated the change in public opinion was the little revolution that took place at the Milhommes' stationery shop. One day Madame Edouard, so long the absolute mistress of the establishment, disappeared into the back shop, where Madame Alexandre had remained so many years. And Madame Alexandre took her place at the counter and served the customers. Nobody mistook the meaning of that revolution,—the customers were changing, the secular school was triumphing over its Congregational rival, and thus, in the interests of the business, Madame Edouard, like a good trader, made way for her sister-in-law. It must be said, too, that Madame Edouard now had some great worries with her son Victor, who, entering the army after his departure from the Brothers' school, and reaching the rank of sergeant, had lately been compromised in a very unpleasant affair; whereas Madame Alexandre had every right to be proud of her son Sébastien, who had been one of Simon's and Marc's best pupils, then Joseph's companion at the Training College, and was now, for three years past, assistant-master at Rouville. Indeed, all those young folk, Sébastien, Joseph, and Louise, after growing up together, had at last reached active life, bringing with them broad minds, ripened early in the midst of tears, to continue the bitterly-contested work of their elders.

A year went by. Louise was now twenty, and, repairing to Jonville every Sunday, spent the day with her parents. She then often met Joseph and Sébastien, who had remained great friends and were very fond of visiting their former masters, Marc and Salvan. It also frequently happened that Joseph was accompanied by his sister Sarah, who was well pleased to spend a day in the open air among her best friends. For three years past she had been residing with her grandparents, the Lehmanns, displaying so much activity and skill that a little prosperity had returned to the dismal shop in the Rue du Trou. Customers had returned to it, and Sarah, retaining the connection formed with some of the large Paris clothiers, had recruited several work girls and banded them together in a kind of co-operative group. Madame Lehmann had lately died, however, and her husband, now seventy-five years old, lingered on with only one regret, which was that his age deprived him of all hope of ever witnessing Simon's rehabilitation. Every year he spent a week or two with Simon, David, and Rachel among the Pyrenees, and returned home well pleased to have found them working quietly in their lonely retreat, but also very sad when he realized that they would know no real happiness as long as the monstrous proceedings of Rozan should remain unrevised. Sarah had tried to induce the old man to stay with the others in the south, but he obstinately returned to the Rue du Trou, under the pretence of making himself useful there by superintending the workroom. And, as it happened, this circumstance enabled the girl to take an occasional holiday when, on accompanying her brother Joseph to Jonville, she chanced to feel somewhat tired.

The reunion of the young people at Jonville, the days they spent there so gaily, brought about the long-foreseen marriages. At first it was a question of Sébastien marrying Sarah, which surprised nobody; though it was regarded as an indication of the changing times that young Milhomme should marry Simon's daughter not only with the consent of his mother but also with the approval of Madame Edouard, his aunt. A little later, when the wedding was postponed for a few months in order that it might coincide with that of Louise and Joseph, a little excitement arose at Maillebois, for this time the proposed union was one between the condemned man's son and the daughter of his most valiant defender. But the idyl of their love, which was the outcome of the old bitter battle and all the heroism that had been displayed in it, touched many a heart, and even tended to pacify the onlookers, though all were curious to learn how Louise's marriage would be regarded by her great-grandmother, Madame Duparque, who, for three years past, had not quitted her little house on the Place des Capucins. And, indeed, the marriage was postponed for another month in order that Madame Duparque might come to some decision respecting it.

Though Louise was now twenty years old, she had not made her first Communion, and it had been settled that only the civil ceremony should be performed at her wedding with Joseph, as at that of Sébastien with Sarah. Anxious as she was for an interview with Madame Duparque, the girl wrote her an entreating letter; but all in vain, for she did not even receive an answer. The old lady's door had not been opened to Geneviève and her children since they had returned to Marc. For nearly five years now the great-grandmother had clung to her fierce oath that she would cast off all her relatives and live cloistered, alone with God. Geneviève, touched by the thought of that woman of fourscore years leading in solitude a life of gloom and silence, had made a few attempts at a *rapprochement*, but they had been savagely, obstinately repulsed. Nevertheless, Louise desired to make a last attempt, distressed as she was at not having the approval of all her kinsfolk in her happiness.

One evening, then, at sunset, she repaired to the little house, which was already steeped in the dimness of twilight. But, to her astonishment, on pulling the bell-knob, she heard no sound; it seemed as if somebody had cut the wire. Gathering courage, she then ventured to knock, at first lightly, and then loudly; and at last she heard a slight noise, the board of a little judas cut in the door, as in the door of a convent, having been pulled aside.

'Is it you, Pélagie?' Louise inquired. 'Is it you? Answer me!'

It was only with difficulty, after placing her ear close to the judas, that she at last heard the servant's deadened and almost unrecognisable voice: 'Go away, go away,' Pélagie answered; 'madame says that you are to go away at once!'

'Well, no, Pélagie, I won't go away,' Louise promptly retorted. 'Go back and tell grandmother that I shall not leave the door until she has come and answered me herself.'

The girl remained waiting for ten minutes, or perhaps a quarter of an hour. From time to time she knocked again—not angrily, but with respectful, solicitous persistence. And all at once the judas was re-opened, but this time in a tempestuous fashion, and a rough, subterranean voice called to her: 'What have you come here for? You wrote to me about a fresh abomination, a marriage, the very shame of which might well suffice to kill me! What is the use of speaking of it? Are you even fit to marry? Have you made your first Communion? No, eh? You amused yourself with me, you were to have made it when you were twenty years old; but to-day, no doubt, you have decided that you will never do so.... So it is useless for you to come here. Be off, I tell you, I am dead to you!'

Louise, quite upset, shuddering as if she had felt an icy breath from the grave sweeping across her cheek, had barely time to cry: 'Grandmother, I will wait a little longer; I will come back in a month's time!' Then the judas was shut violently, and the little dim and silent house became quite deathly in the darkness, which had now gathered all around.

During the previous five years Madame Duparque had gradually relinquished all intercourse with the world. At first, on the morrow of Madame Berthereau's death and Geneviève's departure, she had contented herself with ceasing to receive her relations, restricting herself to the society of a few pious friends of her own sex, and of the priests and other clerics whom she had made her familiars. Among these was Abbé Coquard, who had succeeded Abbé Quandieu at St. Martin's. He was a rigid man, full of a sombre faith, and it delighted Madame Duparque to hear the threats which he addressed to the wicked—threats of hell with its consuming flames, its red forks, and its boiling oil. Thus, morning and evening she was seen repairing now to the parish church, now to the Capuchin Chapel, in order to attend the various offices and ceremonies. But as time went by she went out less and less, and at last a day came when she ceased to cross her threshold. It was as if she were gradually sinking into gloom and silence, burying herself by slow degrees. One day even the shutters of her house, which had still been opened every morning and closed at night, remained closed, the façade becoming blind, as it were, the house dead, neither a glimmer nor a breath of life emanating from it any more. One might have thought that it was abandoned, uninhabited, if sundry frocks and gowns had not been seen slipping through the doorway at nightfall. They were the gowns of Abbé Coquard, Father Théodose, and at times—so people said—Father Crabot, who thus paid the old lady friendly visits. Her little fortune, now a matter of two or three thousand francs a year, which she had arranged to leave, one half to the College of Valmarie, the other to the Capuchin Chapel, hardly sufficed to explain the fidelity of her clerical friends. Their visits must also have been due in part to her exacting and despotic nature, which overcame the most powerful, and in part to their apprehensions of some deed of mystical madness, of which they knew her to be capable. It was said, too, that she had obtained an authorisation to hear Mass and take the Communion at home; and this, no doubt, explained why she no longer set foot out of doors. By the force of her piety she had compelled even the Deity to come to her house, in order that she might be spared the affliction of going to His; for the idea of seeing the streets and the people in them, of again setting her eyes on that abominable age in which Holy Church was agonising, had become such torture to her that she had caused her shutters to be nailed in position, and every chink in the woodwork to be stopped up, in order that no sound or gleam of the world might again reach her.

This was the supreme crisis. She spent her days in prayer. She was not content with having broken off all intercourse with her impious and accursed relations, she asked herself if her own salvation were not in danger through having incurred, perhaps, some responsibility in the damnation of her kinsfolk. She was haunted by a recollection of Madame Berthereau's sacrilegious revolt on her death-bed, and believed that unhappy woman to be not merely in purgatory, but in hell. Then, too, came the thought of Geneviève, whom the demon had assailed so terribly, and who had gone back to her errors like a dog to his vomit. And, finally, there was Louise, the pagan, the godless creature, who had rejected even the gift of the Divine Body of Jesus. Those two—Geneviève and Louise—belonged, both in body and in spirit, to the devil; and if Madame Duparque caused Masses to be said and candles burnt for the repose of her dead daughter's soul, she had abandoned those who still lived to the just wrath of her God of anger and punishment. But, at the same time, her anguish remained extreme; she wondered why Heaven had thus stricken her in her posterity, and strove to interpret this visitation as a terrible trial, whence her own holiness would emerge dazzling and triumphant. The confined, claustral life she led, entirely devoted to religious practices, seemed to her to be necessary reparation, for which she would be rewarded by an eternity of delight. In this wise she expiated the monstrous sinfulness of her descendants, those women guilty of free thought, who, in three generations, had escaped from the Church and ended madly by putting their belief in a religion of human solidarity. Thus, wishing to redeem the apostasy of her grandchildren, Madame Duparque set all her pride in humbling herself, in living for God alone, in seeking to slay what little womanliness still lingered in her; for it was from that womanliness that her condemned descendants had sprung.

So stern and sombre was her ardour that she wearied the few clerics who alone now linked her to the world. She was conscious of the decline of the Church; she could detect the collapse of Catholicism under the efforts of those diabolical times from which she had withdrawn by way of protest against Satan's victory—as if, indeed, she denied that victory by not beholding it. And in her opinion her renunciation, her fancied martyrdom, might perhaps impart new vigour to the soldiers of religion. She would have liked to have seen them as ardent, as resolute, as fierce as she herself was, encasing themselves in the rigidity of dogmas, carrying fire and sword into the midst of the unbelievers, and aiding the great Exterminator to conquer His people by dint of thunderbolts. She never felt satisfied; she found Father Crabot, Father Théodose, even the sombre Abbé Coquard, altogether too lukewarm. She accused them of compounding with the hateful worldly spirit of the times, and of completing the ruin of the Church with their own hands by adapting religion to the tastes of the day. She dictated their duty to them, preached a campaign of frankness and violence, unhinged as she was, thrown into extreme exaltation by her lonely life, and ever athirst with some supreme longings in spite of all the penitence heaped upon her.

Father Crabot was the first to grow tired of that strange penitent, who, at eighty-three years of age, treated herself so harshly, and bore herself like a despairing prophetess, whose uncompromising Catholicism was really a condemnation of the long efforts made by his own Order to humanise the terrible Deity of the stakes and the massacres. Thus the Jesuit allowed long intervals to elapse between his discreet visits, and, finally, he altogether ceased to call, being of opinion, no doubt, that the legacy he had hoped to receive for Valmarie would not be sufficient compensation for the dangers he might incur with a woman whose soul was ever in a tempest. A few months later Abbé Coquard likewise withdrew, not because he had any cowardly fears of being compromised, but because each of his discussions with the old lady degenerated into a horrible battle. Eager and despotic like herself, the Abbé was bent on retaining all his power and authority as a priest; and one day, when Madame Duparque began to thunder in the name of God, reproaching him with inaction, in such wise that he appeared to be a mere transgressing sinner, he became quite angry, for he declined to accept such a reversal of their respective positions. Then, for nearly another year, only Father Théodose's frock was to be seen slipping into the little, silent, closed house of the Place des Capucins.

Father Théodose, no doubt, regarded Madame Duparque's little fortune as worth taking, for the times were hard with poor St. Antony of Padua. In vain did the Capuchin scatter prospectuses broadcast; money did not now flow into the collection boxes as it had done in the happy days when, by a stroke of genius, he had induced Monseigneur Bergerot to bless one of the saint's bones. In those days the miracle lottery had put people into quite a fever; the sick, the idle, and the poor had all dreamt of winning happiness from heaven in return for an investment of twenty sous; whereas, now that a little sense and truth were spreading through the district, thanks to the secular schools, the base commerce of the Capuchin Chapel stood revealed in all its shameful imbecility.

For a time, it is true, another stroke of genius on the part of Father Théodose, the creation of some wonderful mortgage bonds on heaven, had again stirred the souls of the humble and the suffering, who, as life below proved so cruel to them, hungered for felicity beyond the grave. Then, during several months, the money of dupes had flowed in; all the savings hidden in old stockings had been brought forth by believers anxious to secure the chance of a little peace in the Unknown. But finally, being confronted by growing incredulity, Father Théodose had found it difficult to place his remaining bonds, and had thereupon planned a third stroke of genius—this time the invention of some private, reserved gardens in the ever-flowery Fields of the Blessed. According to him there were to be some delightful little nooks in Eternity, garnished with roses and lilies of the very best varieties, under foliage set out to please the eyes, and near springs which would be particularly pure and fresh. And thanks once more to the decisive intervention of St. Antony of Padua, one might book those little nooks in advance, thereby ensuring to oneself the eternal enjoyment of them. Naturally, the booking was very expensive if one desired something spacious and comfortable, though there were indeed gardens at all prices, which varied in accordance with site, charm, and proximity to the abodes of the angels. Two old ladies, it appeared, had already bequeathed their fortunes to the Capuchins in order that the miracle-working saint might reserve for them two of the best gardens that were still vacant, one being in the style of an old French park, whereas the other was more of the 'romantic' type, with a maze and a waterfall. And it was also said that Madame Duparque had in a like way made her choice, this being a golden grotto on the slope of an azure mount, among clumps of myrtle bushes and oleanders.

Father Théodose, then, alone continued to visit the old lady, putting up with her fits of temper, and returning to the house even after she had driven him from it in exasperation at finding him so lukewarm and resigned to the triumph of the Church's enemies. And the Capuchin had actually ended by securing a latch-key in order that he might enter the house whenever he pleased, instead of having to ring the bell again and again, for poor Pélagie had become extremely deaf. It was also at this same moment that the two women, the two recluses as they may be called, cut the bell wire; for of what use was it to retain that connecting link with the outer world? The only living being whom they now received had a key to admit himself, and by cutting the wire they were spared the nervous starts that came upon them whenever they heard that jangling bell which they did not wish to answer. Pélagie, indeed, had become as fierce and as maniacal as her mistress. She had begun by curtailing her chats in the tradespeople's shops, scarcely speaking to anybody when she went out, but gliding swiftly past the houses like a shadow. Next, she had decided to go shopping twice a week only, in this wise condemning her mistress and herself to live on stale bread and a few vegetables—such fare as might have suited a pair of hermits in the desert. And now the few tradespeople came themselves to the house at nightfall on Saturday evenings, and left their goods at the doorway in a basket, which they found waiting for them on the ensuing Saturday, with the money due to them wrapped in a scrap of newspaper.

At the same time Pélagie had one great worry—her nephew Polydor, who had entered a Beaumont monastery in a menial capacity, and who came and made frightful scenes with her whenever he wished to extort money. He alarmed the old woman to such a degree that she did not even dare to leave him at the door, for she felt sure that on some pretext or other he would collect a crowd and force his way in. And when she had admitted him, she trembled still more; for she knew that he was a man to deal her a nasty blow should she refuse to give him a ten-franc piece. For many long years she had caressed the dream of employing all her savings—some ten thousand francs, scraped together copper by copper—to procure some happiness in the other world; and if the little treasure was still carefully hidden away inside her palliasse, this was because she hesitated as to the best, the most efficacious mode of investment. Should she found a perpetual Mass for the repose of her soul, or should she book one of Father Théodose's reserved gardens, a modest little nook in heaven, by the side of her mistress's lordly grotto? And she was still hesitating in this respect when misfortune fell upon her.

One night, when she had been obliged to admit Polydor, the rascal did not murder her, but rushed in turn upon every article of furniture in her garret, finally ripping up the palliasse and fleeing with the ten thousand francs, while Pélagie, whom he had thrust aside and who had fallen beside the bed, groaned with despair at seeing that bandit—who was of her own flesh and blood—make off with the blessed money which St. Antony of Padua was to have given her back in eternal delight. Would she be damned, then, as she no longer possessed the wherewithal to speculate in the miraculous lottery? Such was the shock the old woman experienced that two days later she died; and it was Father Théodose who found her, already stark and cold, in her bare and dirty garret, to which he climbed in his surprise and anxiety at discovering her nowhere else. He was obliged to attend to everything—declare the death, make arrangements for the funeral, and busy himself as to how the last remaining inmate of the little house would live now that she had nobody left to serve her.

For several weeks past Madame Duparque, whose legs had become too feeble to support her weight, had taken to her bed, in which, however, she remained in a sitting posture, erect and tall, though withered. Little breath was left her, yet she still seemed to reign despotically over that silent, dark, and empty house, whence she had driven all her kith and kin, and where the only creature, the domestic animal, whom she had been willing to tolerate, had just died. When Father Théodose, on returning from Pélagie's funeral, tried to ascertain Madame Duparque's intentions with respect to her future mode of life, he could not even extract an answer from her. Greatly embarrassed, he insisted, and offered to send her a sister, pointing out that it was impossible for her to attend to any household duties as she could not even leave her bed. But she at once flew into a temper, growled like some mighty animal stricken unto death and unwilling to be disturbed in its final hour. Vague charges gurgled in her throat; they were all cowards, all traitors to their God, all egotists who abandoned the Church in order that the vaults might not fall upon their heads! Thereupon Father Théodose, in his turn growing exasperated, left her, deciding that he would return the following morning to see if she had become more reasonable.

A night and a day elapsed, for the Superior of the Capuchins was only able to return at dusk, four and twenty hours later. During that night and day, then, Madame Duparque remained alone, absolutely alone, behind the nailed shutters, the carefully closed doors and windows of her dark room, where neither a sound nor a ray of light from the outer world penetrated. She herself had willed it thus, severing all carnal ties with her relations, withdrawing from the world in protest against the hateful society of the times in which sin had proved triumphant. And, after giving herself wholly to the Church, she had gradually become disgusted with its ministers—those priests who lacked all militant faith, those monks who had no heroic bravery, but who were all worldly men bent on personal enjoyment. Thus she had dismissed them also, and now she remained alone with her Deity—an implacable and stubborn Deity, who ruled with absolute, exterminating, and vengeful power. All light and all life had departed from that cold, dismal, fast-closed, and tomb-like house, where there only remained a feeble octogenarian woman, sitting up in bed, gazing into the black darkness, and waiting for her jealous God to carry her away, in order that lukewarm souls might have an example of a really pious end. And when Father Théodose presented himself at the house at dusk he found, to his intense surprise, that the door would not open, that it resisted all his efforts. The key turned readily enough in the lock, and it seemed, therefore, that the door must have been bolted. But who could have bolted it? There was nobody inside except the ailing woman, who could not leave her bed. The Capuchin then made fresh attempts, but in vain; and at last, feeling frightened, unwilling to incur any further responsibility, he hastened to the Town Hall to explain the matter to the authorities. A messenger was at once sent to Mademoiselle Mazeline's for Louise; and, as it happened, Marc and Geneviève were there, having come over from Jonville as the news of Pélagie's death had made them feel anxious.

A tragical business followed. The whole family repaired to the Place des Capucins. As the door would not yield, a locksmith was sent for, but he declared he could do nothing, for assuredly the bolts were fastened. It therefore became necessary to send for a mason, who, with his pick, unsealed the door hinges set in the stone work. At each blow the silent house re-echoed like a closed vault. And when the door had been torn down it was with a quiver that Marc and Geneviève, followed by Louise, re-entered that family abode whence they had been banished. An icy dampness reigned there; it was only with difficulty that they managed to light a candle. And upstairs, in the bed, they found Madame Duparque, still in a sitting posture, propped up by pillows, but quite dead, with a large crucifix between her long, thin, shrivelled hands.

In a superhuman effort she had assuredly found the supreme energy to leave her bed, crawl down the stairs, and shoot the bolts in order that no living soul, not even a priest, might disturb her in her last communion with God. And then she had crawled upstairs again, and had died there. When Father Théodose saw her he fell on his knees, shuddering, and stammering a prayer. He was distraught, for he detected in that death not merely the end of a terrible old woman, raised to a fierce grandeur, as it were, by her uncompromising faith, but also the end of all superstitious and mendacious religion. And Marc, in whose arms Geneviève and Louise had sought a refuge, seemed to feel a great gust sweeping by, as though eternal life were springing from that death.

When the family, after leaving the funeral arrangements to Abbé Coquard, made a search in the old lady's drawers, they found nothing—neither will nor securities of any kind. It could not be said that Father Théodose had purloined any property, for he had not returned to the house. Was it to be assumed, then, that the old lady had previously handed her securities to him or to another? Or had she destroyed them, unwilling that her relatives should benefit by her fortune? The mystery was never solved, not a copper was ever found. Only the little house remained, and it was sold, the proceeds being given to the poor at the request of Geneviève, who said that in taking that course she was certainly doing what her grandmother would have desired.

In the evening, after returning from the funeral, Geneviève cast her arms round her husband's neck, and made him a frank confession: 'If you only knew!' said she. 'I was beset again when I heard that grandmother was all alone, so bravely and loftily adhering to her stubborn faith.... Yes, I asked myself if my place were not beside her, and if I had done right in leaving her.... But what can you expect, dear? I shall never be quite cured. In the depths of my being I shall always retain a little of my old belief.... Yet, what a frightful death that was! And how right you are in asking that people should live as they ought to; that women should be liberated, set in their right position as the equals and companions of men, and that life should partake of all that is good and true and just!'

A month later the two long-deferred weddings at last took place. Louise was married to Joseph, Sarah to Sébastien; and in those espousals Marc perceived a beginning of victory. The good crop, sown with so much difficulty in the midst of persecution and outrage, was germinating and growing already.

CHAPTER II

Years went by, and Marc continued his work, sturdy yet at sixty years of age, and as passionately attached to truth and justice as he had been at the outset of the great struggle. And one day, when he happened to go to Beaumont to call on Delbos, the latter suddenly said to him: 'By the way, my dear fellow, I have had a strange encounter.... The other evening, at dusk, while I was returning home I noticed a man of about your age, looking wretched and ravaged, walking ahead of me along the Avenue des Jaffres.... And, all at once, in the blaze of light coming from the confectioner's shop at the corner of the Rue Gambetta, it seemed to me that I recognised our Gorgias.'

'Eh, our Gorgias?'

'Why, yes, Brother Gorgias, not wearing an Ignorantine's cassock, but a greasy frock-coat, and slipping alongside the walls, with the suspicious gait of an emaciated old wolf.... He must have come back secretly, and must be living in some dark nook or other, still trying to frighten and exploit his old accomplices.'

Marc, whom the announcement had greatly surprised, remained full of doubt. 'You must have been mistaken,' said he; 'Gorgias attaches too much value to his skin to return to Beaumont and run the risk of being sent to the galleys—that is whenever the discovery of a new fact may enable us to apply for the quashing of the Rozan judgment.'

'It is you who are mistaken, my friend,' Delbos answered. 'Our man has nothing more to fear. According to our law of limitation there can be no public action in a criminal matter after the expiration of ten years, and so, even nowadays, little Zéphirin's murderer can walk the streets in the daylight without any fear of arrest.... However, I may have been deceived by a mere resemblance; and in any case the return of Gorgias can have no interest for us, for you agree with me, do you not, that we can derive nothing useful from him?'

'No, nothing whatever. He lied so much at the time of the affair that if he should say anything now he would certainly lie again.... The long-sought truth can never come to us from him.'

In this wise, at long intervals, Marc called upon Delbos in order to chat with him about that everlasting Simon case, which, after the lapse of so many years, still remained like a cancer gnawing at the heart of the country. People might deny its existence, believe it to be dead, cease to speak of it, but nevertheless it still stealthily prosecuted its ravages, like some secret venom poisoning life. Twice a year David quitted his lonely retreat in the Pyrenees and came to Beaumont in order to confer with Delbos and Marc; for, in spite of the pardon granted to his brother, he had not for an hour relinquished his hope of eventual acquittal and rehabilitation. They, David, Delbos, and Marc, were convinced that the monstrous verdict would be some day set aside, and that the affair would end by the victory of the innocent. But, even as in previous years, after the judgment of the Court of Cassation, they found themselves struggling amidst an intricate network of falsehoods. After hesitating for a time as to which scent they might best follow, they had decided to investigate a second crime committed by ex-President Gragnon, a crime which they had already suspected at Rozan, and of which they were now convinced.

Gragnon, at the time of the Rozan proceedings, had repeated his illegal communication trick. On this second occasion, however, he had availed himself, not of one of Simon's letters with a forged postscript and paraph, but of a confession alleged to have been written by the workman who was said to have made a false stamp for the Maillebois schoolmaster—this confession having been handed, it was alleged, to one of the nuns of the Beaumont hospital by the workman in question when he was near his death. Assuredly Gragnon had walked about Beaumont with that confession in his pocket, speaking of it as a thunderbolt which he would hurl at the Simonists if they drove him to extremities, showing it also, or causing it to be shown, to certain members of the jury, those who were pious and weak-minded, but at the same time affecting a keen desire to save the holy nun to whom the confession had been given from being publicly mixed up in such a scandal. And this explained everything. The abominable behaviour of the jury in reconvicting the innocent prisoner became excusable. Those men of average intelligence and honesty had been deceived like the jurors of Beaumont, and had yielded to motives which had remained secret. Marc and David well remembered that they had heard some juryman ask certain questions which had then seemed to them ridiculous. But they now understood that this juryman had referred to the terrible document which Gragnon had stealthily hawked about, and of which it was not prudent to speak plainly. Delbos therefore busied himself with that new fact, that second criminal communication, which, if proved, would entail the immediate annulment of the proceedings at Rozan. But, unfortunately, nothing could be more difficult to prove, and for years Delbos and his friends had striven vainly. Only one hope remained to them: a juror, a retired medical man, named Beauchamp, had acquired a certainty that the workman's alleged confession was simply a gross forgery. In a measure things repeated themselves, as is not infrequently the case in real life, Beauchamp being assailed by remorse like his predecessor, architect Jacquin. He himself, it is true, was not a clerical, but he had an extremely devout wife and did not wish to plunge her into desolation by relieving his conscience. Thus it was necessary to wait. [1]

However, as the years went by, circumstances became more favourable. Thanks to the spread of secular education the social evolution was being hastened and giving great results. All France was being renewed, a new nation was coming from its thousands of parish schools, whose influence was to be found beneath each fresh reform that was effected, each fresh step that was taken toward solidarity and peace. Things which had seemed impossible in former times were easily accomplished now that the nation was delivered from error and falsehood, endowed with knowledge and force of will.

> [1] It may be held that M. Zola has perpetrated an artistic blunder by introducing into his narrative a repetition, so to say, of the Jacquin episode; but it should be remembered that the Simon affair is based on the Dreyfus case, in which there were several repetitions of that character. Among those who sat in judgment on Dreyfus, Esterhazy, and Picquart, there were repeated instances of belated conscientious scruples, some indeed known to the initiated but never made public. Thus, if M. Zola is inartistic in making two characters of his story adopt virtually the same course, he is at least true to life.—*Trans.*

Thus, at the general elections which took place in May that year, Delbos at last defeated Lemarrois, who had been Mayor of Beaumont for so long a period. At one time it had seemed as if the latter would never lose his seat, personifying as he did the great mass of average public opinion. But the *bourgeoisie* had denied its revolutionary past, and allied itself with the Church in order that it might not have to abandon any of its usurped power. It clung to the privileges it had acquired, and, rather than share its royalty or its wealth with the masses, it preferred to make use of all the old reactionary forces in order to thrust the now awakened and enlightened people into servitude once more. Lemarrois was a typical example of the *bourgeois* Republican, who, wishing to defend his class, sank into a kind of involuntary reaction, and was therefore condemned and swept away in the inevitable *débâcle* of that *bourgeoisie* which a hundred years of trafficking and enjoyment had sufficed to rot. It was inevitable that the people should ascend to power as soon as it became conscious of its strength, of the inexhaustible reserve of energy, intelligence, and will slumbering within it; and it was sufficient that it should be emancipated, roused from the heavy sleep of ignorance by the schools in order that it might take its due place and rejuvenate the nation. The *bourgeoisie* was now at the point of death, and the people would necessarily become the great liberating, justice-dealing France of to-morrow. And there was, so to say, an annunciation of all those things in the victory achieved at Beaumont by Delbos, the man who had been Simon's counsel, who had been denied and insulted so long, at first securing only a few Socialist votes, which by degrees had become an overwhelming majority.

Another proof of the people's accession to power was to be found in the complete change which had come over Marcilly. He had formerly figured in a Radical ministry; then, after the reconviction of Simon, he had entered a Moderate administration; and now he affected extreme Socialist principles; and, by harnessing himself to Delbos's triumphal car, had managed to get re-elected. It is true that the popular victory was not complete throughout the department, for Count Hector de Sanglebœuf had also been re-elected, this time as an uncompromising reactionary; for the usual phenomenon of troublous times had appeared, only plain, frank, extreme opinions finding support. The party vanquished for ever was the old Liberal *bourgeoisie*, which had become Conservative from egotism and fright, and which, lacking all strength and logic, was ripe for its fall. And the ascending class, the great mass of those who only the day before had been called the disinherited, would naturally take the place of the *bourgeoisie* after sweeping away the few stubborn defenders that remained to the Church.

But the election of Delbos was particularly notable as being the first great success achieved by one of those rascals without God or country, one of those traitors who had publicly declared Simon to be innocent. After the monstrous proceedings of Rozan all the notable Simonists had suffered in their persons or their pockets for having dared to desire truth and justice. Insult, persecution, summary dismissal had been heaped upon them. There was Delbos, to whom no client had dared to confide his interests; there was Salvan dismissed, compulsorily retired; there was Marc disgraced, sent to a little village; and behind the leaders how many others there were, relations and friends, who for merely behaving in an upright manner were assailed with worries, and at times even ruined!

Full of mute grief at the sight of such aberration, well understanding that all rebellion was useless, the friends of truth had simply turned to their work, awaiting the inevitable hour when reason and equity would triumph. And that hour seemed to be approaching; for now Delbos, one of the most deeply involved in the affair, had defeated Lemarrois, who had long pursued a pusillanimous policy, refusing to take sides either for or against Simon. Was not this a proof that opinion had changed, that a great advance had been effected? Moreover, Salvan secured consolation, for one of his old pupils was appointed to the directorship of the Training College after Mauraisin had been virtually dismissed for incapacity. Great was the delight of the sage when those tidings reached him, not because it pleased him to crow over his vanquished adversary, but because he at last saw the continuation of his work entrusted to one who was brave and faithful. And, finally, a day came when Le Barazer, who now felt strong enough to repair former injustice, sent for Marc and offered him the head mastership of a school at Beaumont. Such an offer, on the part of that prudent diplomatist, the Academy Inspector, was extremely significant, and Marc was pleased indeed; nevertheless he declined it, for he did not wish to leave Jonville, where his task was not yet finished.

There were also other precursory signs of the great impending change in the country. Prefect Hennebise had been replaced by a very energetic and sensible functionary who had immediately demanded the revocation of Depinvilliers, under whose management the Lycée of Beaumont had become a kind of seminary. Rector Forbes had been compelled to rouse himself from the study of ancient history, in order to dismiss the chaplains, rid the classrooms of the religious emblems placed in them, and secularise secondary as well as elementary education. Then General Jarousse, having been placed on the retired list, had decided to quit Beaumont; for, though his wife owned a house there, he was exasperated with the new spirit which reigned in the town, and did not wish to come into contact with his successor, a Republican general, whom some people even declared to be a Socialist. Moreover, ex-investigating Magistrate Daix had met a wretched death, haunted as he was by spectres, in spite of his belated confession at Rozan; while the former Procureur de la République, Raoul de La Bissonnière, after having a fine career in Paris, seemed likely to come to grief there amidst the collapse of a colossal swindle[2] which he had in some way befriended. And, as a last and excellent symptom of the times, nobody now saluted Gragnon, the ex-presiding judge, when, thin and yellow, he anxiously threaded the Avenue des Jaffres, hanging his head but glancing nervously to right and left as if he feared that somebody might spit upon him as he passed.

> [2] All newspaper readers know that various judicial personages have been compromised in recent French swindles.—*Trans.*

The happy effects of free and secular education, which brought light and health in its train, were also manifest at Maillebois, whither Marc often repaired to see his daughter Louise, who, with Joseph her husband, lived in the little lodging which Mignot had so long occupied at the Communal school. Maillebois, indeed, was no longer that intensely clerical little town, where the Congregations had succeeded in raising their creature Philis to the mayoralty. In former times the eight hundred working men of the *faubourg*, being divided among themselves, could return only a few Republicans to the Municipal Council, in which they were reduced to inaction. But at the recent elections the whole Republican and Socialist list had passed, by a large majority, in such wise that Darras, defeating his rival Philis, had now again become Mayor. And his delight at returning to that office, whence the priests had driven him, was the keener as he was now supported by a compact majority which would enable him to act frankly instead of being continually reduced to compromises.

Marc met Darras one day and found him quite radiant. 'Yes, I remember,' said he, 'you did not think me very brave in former times. That poor Simon! I was convinced of his innocence, yet I refused to act when you came to me at the municipal offices. But how could I help it? I had a bare majority of two, the council constantly escaped my control, and the proof is that it ended by overthrowing me.... Ah! if I had then only had the majority we now possess! We are the masters at last, and things will move quickly, I promise you.'

Marc smiled and asked him what had become of Philis, his defeated adversary.

'Philis—oh! he has been greatly tried. A certain person—you know whom I mean—died recently, and so he has had to resign himself to living alone with his daughter Octavie, a very pious young woman who does not care to marry. His son Raymond, being a naval officer, is always far away, and the house cannot be very cheerful, unless indeed Philis is already seeking consolation, which may be the case, for I saw a new servant there the other day—yes, quite a sturdy, fresh-looking girl!'

Darras burst into a loud laugh. For his own part, having retired from business with a handsome fortune, he was living his last years in perfect union with his wife, their only regret being that they had no children.

'Well,' Marc resumed, 'Joulic may now feel certain that he will not be worried any more.... It is he, you know, who, in spite of all difficulties, transformed the town with his school, and made your election possible.'

'Oh! you were the first great worker,' Darras exclaimed. 'I don't forget the immense services which you rendered.... But you may be quite easy,

Joulic is now safe from all vexations, and I will help him as much as I can in his efforts to make Maillebois free and intelligent.... Besides, your daughter Louise and Simon's son Joseph are now, in their turn, continuing the work of liberation. You are a knot of brave but modest workers, to whom we shall all feel very grateful hereafter.'

Then, for a moment, they chatted about the now distant times when Marc had been first appointed to the Maillebois school. More than thirty years had elapsed! And how many were the events that had occurred, and how many were the children who had passed through the schoolroom and carried some of the new spirit into the district around them! Marc recalled some of his old, his first, pupils. Fernand Bongard, the little peasant with the hard nut, who had married Lucille Doloir, an intelligent girl, whom Mademoiselle Rouzaire had tried to rear in sanctimonious fashion, was now the father of a girl eleven years of age, named Claire, whom Mademoiselle Mazeline was freeing somewhat from clerical servitude. Then Auguste Doloir, the mason's undisciplined son, who had married Angèle Bongard, an obstinate young woman of narrow ambition, had a son of fifteen, Adrien, a remarkably intelligent youth whom Joulic, his master, greatly praised. Charles Doloir, the locksmith, who had been as bad a pupil as his brother, but who had improved somewhat since his marriage with his master's daughter, Marthe Dupuis, also had a son, Marcel, who was now thirteen, and had left the school with excellent certificates. There was also Léon Doloir, who, thanks to Marc, had taken to the teaching profession, and after becoming one of Salvan's best students, now directed the school at Les Bordes, assisted by his wife, Juliette Hochard, who had quitted the Training School at Fontenay with 'No. I' against her name. That young couple was all health and good sense, and their life was brightened by the presence of a little four-year-old urchin, Edmond, who was sharp for his age, already knowing his letters thoroughly. Then came the twin Savins: first Achille, so sly, so addicted to falsehoods as a boy, then placed with a process-server, dulled like his father by years of office work, and married to a colleague's sister, Virginie Deschamps, a lean and insignificant *blonde*, by whom he had a charming little girl, Léontine, who at eleven years of age had just secured her certificate, and was one of Mademoiselle Mazeline's favourite pupils. Then came Philippe Savin, who, long remaining without employment, had been rendered better by a life of hardship, and was now still a bachelor, and manager of a model farm, being associated in that enterprise with his younger brother Jules, the most intelligent of the two, who had given himself to the soil and married a peasant girl, Rosalie Bonin—their firstborn, Pierre, now six years old, having lately entered Joulic's school. Thus generation followed generation, each going towards increase of knowledge, reason, truth, and justice, and it was assuredly from that constant evolution which education produced, that the happiness of the communities of the future would spring.

But Marc was more particularly interested in the home of Louise and Joseph, and in that of his dearest pupil, Sébastien Milhomme, who had married Sarah. That day, on quitting Darras, he repaired to the Communal school in order to see his daughter. Mademoiselle Mazeline, now more than sixty years of age, with a record of forty years spent in elementary teaching, had, like Salvan, lately retired to Jonville, where she now dwelt in a very modest little house near his beautiful garden. She might still have rendered some services in her profession had not her eyesight failed her. Indeed, she was nearly blind. In retiring, however, she at least had the consolation of handing her duties over to her well-loved assistant Louise, who was appointed head mistress in her stead. Moreover, a headmastership at Beaumont was now being spoken of for Joulic, in such wise that his assistant Joseph might succeed him at Maillebois; and thus the young couple would share the school which still re-echoed the names of Simon and Marc, whose good work they would continue. Louise, who was now two and thirty, had presented her husband with a son, François, who at twelve years of age was already wonderfully like his grandfather Marc. And the ambition of that big bright-eyed boy with the lofty brow was to enter the Training College like his forerunners, for he also wished to become an elementary teacher.

It was a Thursday—half-holiday day—and Marc found Louise just quitting a housework class which she held once a week outside the regulation hours. Joseph, with his son and some other boys, had gone on a geological and botanical ramble along the banks of the Verpille. But Sarah happened to be with Louise, for she was very much attached to her sister-in-law, and always visited her when she came over from Rouville, where her husband Sébastien was now head-master.

They had a charming little girl, Thérèse, in whom all the beauty of her grandmother Rachel had reappeared. And three times a week Sarah came from Rouville to Maillebois—the journey by rail lasting barely ten minutes—in order to superintend the tailoring business which was still carried on at old Lehmann's in the Rue du Trou. He was now very old indeed, more than eighty, and as it had become difficult for Sarah to superintend the establishment she thought of disposing of it.

As soon as Marc had kissed Louise he pressed both of Sarah's hands. 'And how is my faithful Sébastien?' he asked. 'How is your big girl Thérèse, and how are you yourself, my dear?'

'Everybody is in the best of health,' Sarah answered gaily. 'Even grandfather Lehmann is as strong as an oak-tree in spite of his advanced years.... And I have had good news from yonder, you know. Uncle David has written to say that my father has got over the attacks of fever which have been troubling him occasionally.'

Marc jogged his head gently. 'Yes, yes, his wound is not altogether healed. To restore him completely to health one needs that long-desired rehabilitation which it is so difficult to obtain. We are advancing towards it, however; I am still full of hope, for glorious times are coming.... Remind Sébastien that each boy he makes a man of will be another worker in the cause of truth and justice.'

Then Marc chatted a while with Louise, giving her news of Mademoiselle Mazeline, who lived a very retired life at Jonville in the company of birds and flowers. And he made his daughter promise to send her son François to spend the Sunday there, for it was a great delight for his grandmother to have the boy with her occasionally. 'And why not come yourself?' he added. 'Tell Joseph to come as well; we will all call on Salvan, who will be well pleased to see such a gathering of teachers, whose father in a measure he is.... And you, Sarah, you ought to come with Sébastien and your daughter Thérèse. Let it be a general outing and our pleasure will be complete.... Come, it is understood, eh? Till Sunday, then!'

He kissed the two young women and hurried away, for he wished to catch the six-o'clock train. But he nearly missed it by reason of a strange encounter which for a moment delayed him. He was turning out of the High Street into the avenue leading to the railway station, when he espied two individuals who were disputing violently behind a clump of spindle trees. One of them, who seemed to be a man of forty, attracted Marc's attention by his long, livid, and doltish face. Where was it that he had previously seen that stupid, vicious countenance? All at once he remembered: that man was certainly Polydor, Pélagie's nephew. For more than twenty years Marc had not met him, but he was aware that he had been dismissed, long ago, from the Beaumont convent which he had entered as a servant, and that he led a chance existence among the knaves of disreputable neighbourhoods. However, Polydor, noticing and probably recognising the bystander who was looking at him so attentively, hastened to lead his companion away. And then, as Marc glanced at the other man, he started with surprise. Clad in a dirty frock-coat, looking both wretched and fierce, Polydor's companion had the haggard countenance of an old bird of prey. Surely he was Brother Gorgias! Marc at once remembered what Delbos had told him; and thereupon, wishing to arrive at a certainty, he started after the two men, who had already turned into a little side street. But though he gave the street a good look, he could see nobody. Polydor and the other had disappeared into one of the houses of suspicious aspect which lined it. Then Marc again began to doubt. Was it really Gorgias whom he had seen? He was not prepared to swear it; he feared that he had perhaps yielded to some fancy.

At present Marc triumphed at Jonville. By degrees, as healthy and reasonable men had emerged from his school, the mentality of the region had improved, and not only was there increase of knowledge, logic, frankness, and brotherliness, but great material prosperity was appearing, for a land's fortune and happiness depend solely upon the mental culture and the civic morality of its inhabitants. Again, then, was abundance returning to clean and well-kept homes; the fields, thanks to newly adopted methods of culture, displayed magnificent crops; the countryside was once more becoming a joy for the eyes in the bright summer sunshine. And thus a happy stretch of land was at last advancing towards that perpetual peace which for centuries had been so ardently desired.

Martineau the Mayor, followed by the whole parish council, now acted in agreement with Marc. A series of incidents had hastened that good understanding by which all desirable reforms were accelerated. Abbé Cognasse, after for some time restraining himself, in accordance with the advice given him at Valmarie, which was to retain his influence over the women,—for whoever possesses their support proves invincible,—had relapsed into his wonted violence, incapable as he was of long remaining patient, and enraged, too, at seeing the women gradually escape from him, owing to the ill grace with which he sought to detain them. At last, like the vengeful minister of a ravaging and exterminating Deity, he became absolutely brutal, distributing outrageous punishment in his wrath at the slightest offences. One day, for instance, he rubbed little Moulin's ears till they positively bled, merely because the lad had playfully pulled the skirts of the terrible Palmyre, who, in her time, had administered smacks and whippings so freely. Another day the Abbé boxed young Catherine's ears in church because she laughed during Mass on seeing him blow his nose at the altar. And finally, one Sunday, quite beside himself at finding that the district was escaping from his control, he actually launched a kick at Madame Martineau the mayoress, imagining that she defied him because she did not make room for him to pass as quickly as he desired. This time it was held that his behaviour exceeded all bounds, and Martineau, quite enraged, cited him before the Tribunal of Correctional Police, with the result that the battle became a furious one, Cognasse retaliating with fresh acts of violence, and gathering quite a quantity of lawsuits around him.

Marc meanwhile, anxious to complete his work in the village, had been nursing an idea, which he was at last able to carry into effect. In consequence of some new laws enacted by the Legislature, the Sisters of the Good Shepherd, who carried on the factory in which two hundred work-girls were sweated and starved, had been obliged to quit Jonville. And it was a good riddance for the district, a plague-spot, a shame the less. Marc, however, persuaded the parish council to purchase the large factory buildings, when they were offered for sale by auction; his idea being to modify and turn them into a Common House, in which recreation and dancing rooms, a library, a museum, and even some free baths might be gradually installed as by degrees the resources of the parish increased. In this wise he dreamt of setting, in full view of the church, a kind of civic palace, which would become a meeting and recreation place for the hard-working community. If the women for years past had only continued to go to Mass in order to show their new gowns and see those of their acquaintances, they would yet more willingly repair to that cheerful palace of solidarity, where a little healthy amusement would await them. Thus, the recreation rooms were the first inaugurated, and the ceremony gave rise to a great popular demonstration.

The desire of the inhabitants was to efface and redeem that former consecration of the parish to the Sacred Heart, which had filled the mayor and the council with keen remorse ever since they had recovered their senses. Martineau, for his part, accounted for that proceeding by accusing Jauffre of having abandoned him to Abbé Cognasse, after disturbing his mind by threatening both the parish and himself with all sorts of misfortunes if he did not submit to the Church, which would always be the most powerful of the social forces. Martineau, who now perceived that this was not correct, for the Church was already being beaten, and the more the district drew away from it the more prosperous it became, was very desirous of setting himself on the winning side, like a practical peasant, one who talked little but who always kept his eye fixed on the main chance. He would therefore have liked some kind of abjuration, some ceremony such as might allow him to come forward at the head of the council, and restore the parish to the worship of reason and truth, in order to wipe out that former ceremony when it had dedicated itself to dementia and falsehood. And it was this desire which Marc thought of fulfilling by arranging that the mayor and the council should in a fitting manner inaugurate the recreation rooms of the new Common House, in which it was proposed that the inhabitants of the district should meet every Sunday to take part in suitable civic festivities.

Great preparations were made. It was arranged that the pupils of Marc and Geneviève should act a little play, dance, and sing. An orchestra was soon recruited among the young men of the region. Maidens clad in white were also to sing and dance in honour of the work of the fields and the joys of life. Indeed it was particularly life, lived healthily and fully, overflowing with duties and felicities, that was to be celebrated as the universal source of strength and certainty. And the various games and recreations which had been provided, games of skill and energy, gymnastic appliances, with running tracks and lawns set out in the adjoining grounds, were to be handed over to the young folk who would meet there every week, while shady nooks would be reserved for wives and mothers, who would be drawn together and enlivened by having a *salon*, a meeting place, assigned to them. For the inaugural ceremony, the rooms were decorated with flowers and foliage, and already at an early hour the inhabitants of Jonville, clad in their Sunday best, filled the village streets with their mirth.

By Marc's desire, and with the consent of the parents, Mignot, that Sunday, brought his pupils over from Le Moreux in order that they might participate in the festivity. He was met by Marc near the church just as old Palmyre double-locked the door of the edifice in a violent, wrathful fashion. That morning Abbé Cognasse had said Mass to empty benches, and it was he who, in a fit of furious anger, had ordered his servant to close the church. Nobody should enter it again, said he, as those impious people were bent on offering sacrifices to the idols of human bestiality. He himself had disappeared, hiding away in the parsonage whose garden wall bordered the road leading to the new Common House.

'This is the second Sunday that he has not gone to Le Moreux,' Mignot said to Marc. 'He declares with some truth that it is not worth his while to trudge so many miles to say Mass in the presence of two old women and three little girls. The whole village has rebelled against him, you know, since he brutally spanked little Eugénie Louvard for having put out her tongue to him; though that is only one of the acts of violence in which he has indulged since he has felt himself to be defeated. Curiously enough, it is I who am obliged to defend him now for fear lest the indignant villagers should do him an injury.'

Mignot laughed and, on being questioned, gave further particulars. 'Yes, Saleur, our mayor, has talked of bringing an action against him and writing to his bishop. As a matter of fact, if I at first had some difficulty in extricating Le Moreux from the ignorance and credulity in which it was steeped by my predecessor Chagnat, at present I simply have to let events follow their course. The whole population is rallying around me, the school will soon reign without a rival, for, as the church is being shut up, the battle is virtually over.'

'Oh! we have not got to that point yet,' Marc answered. 'Here, at Jonville, Cognasse will resist till the last moment—that is, as long as he is paid by the State and imposed on us by Rome. But I have often thought that the lonely little hamlets like Le Moreux, particularly when life is easy there, would be the first to free themselves from the priests, because the latter's departure would make virtually no alteration in their social life. When people don't like their priest, when they go to church less and less, the disappearance of the priest is witnessed without regret.'

However, Marc and Mignot could not linger chatting any longer, for the ceremony would soon begin. So they repaired to the Common House, where their pupils had now assembled. They there found Geneviève with Salvan and Mademoiselle Mazeline, both the latter having emerged from their retirement to attend that festival which was, so to say, their work, the celebration of their teaching. And everything passed off in a very simple, fraternal, and joyous manner. The authorities, Martineau wearing his scarf of office at the head of the council, took possession of that little Palace of the People in the name of the parish. Then the schoolchildren acted, played, and sang, inaugurating, as it were, the future of happy peace and beneficent work with their healthy and innocent hands. It was, indeed, ever-reviving youth, it was the children, who would overcome the last obstacles on the road to the future city of perfect solidarity. That which the child of to-day had been unable to do would be done by the child of to-morrow. And when the little ones had raised their cry of hope, the youths and the maidens came forward, displaying the promise of early fruitfulness. One found, too, maturity and harvest in all the assembled fathers and mothers, behind whom were the old folk typifying the happy evening which attends life when it has been lived as it should be lived. And all were now acquiring a true consciousness of things, setting their ideal no longer in any mysticism, but in the proper regulation of human life, which needed to be all reason, truth, and justice in order that mankind might dwell together in peace, brotherliness, and happiness. Henceforth Jonville would have a meeting hall in that fraternal house where joy and health would take the place of threat and punishment, where enlightenment would gladden the hearts of one and all. No heart nor mind would be disturbed there by mystical impostures, no shares in any false paradise would be offered for sale. Those who came forth from that building would be cheerful citizens, happy to live for the sake of the joy of life. And all the cruel and grotesque absurdity of dogmas would crumble in the presence of that simple gaiety, that beneficent light.

The dancing lasted until the evening. Never had the comely peasant women of Jonville participated in such a festival. Everybody noticed the radiant countenance of Madame Martineau, who had remained one of

Abbé Cognasse's last worshippers, though, in reality, she had only gone to church in order to show off her new gowns. She wore a new gown that day, and was delighted at being able to display it without any fear that it might become soiled by trailing over damp and dirty flagstones. Again, she knew that she ran no risk of being kicked if she did not get soon enough out of somebody's way. Briefly, in that Common House Jonville would at last have a fitting *salon* where one and all might freely meet and chat, and even indulge in a little harmless coquetry.

But it so happened that an extraordinary incident marked the close of that great day. Marc and Geneviève were escorting their pupils homeward, with Mignot, who also had marshalled his children together; and Salvan and Mademoiselle Mazeline likewise figured in the party, which was all gaiety, jest, and laughter. Near by, too, there was Madame Martineau, accompanied by a group of women, to whom she recounted the result of the legal proceedings which her husband had brought against the priest for kicking her. Fifteen witnesses had given evidence before the Court, and after some uproarious proceedings Abbé Cognasse had been sentenced to a fine of five and twenty francs, this being the chief cause of the fury which he had displayed for several days past. And, all at once, as Madame Martineau—finishing her narrative as she passed the parsonage garden—remarked that the fine was no more than the priest deserved, Abbé Cognasse in person popped his head over the garden wall and began to vociferate insults.

'Ah! you vain hussy!' he cried, 'you lying thing! how dare you spit on God? I'll force your serpent tongue back into your throat!'

How was it that the priest happened to be there at that particular moment? Nobody could tell. Perhaps he had been waiting behind the wall for the return of the villagers. Perhaps he had set a ladder in readiness in order that he might climb and look over. At all events, when he perceived La Martineau in her new gown, surrounded by a number of other sprucely dressed women, who had deserted the church to attend an impious ceremony in the devil's house, he completely lost his head.

'You shameless creatures, you make the very angels weep!' he shouted. 'You cursed creatures, you poison the whole district with your filth! But wait, wait a moment, I will settle your accounts for you without waiting for Satan to come and take you!'

And forthwith, exasperated as he was at no longer having even the women with him,—those unhappy, feared, and execrated women whom the Church captures and employs as its instruments,—he tore some stones from the ruined coping of the wall and flung them with his lean dark hands at Madame Martineau and her companions.

'That's one for you, La Mathurine!' he shouted. 'I know of your goings on with your husband's farm hands!... That's one for you, La Durande! You robbed your sister of her share of your father's property.... And here's for you, La Désirée! You haven't yet paid for the three Masses which I said for the repose of your child's soul!... And as for you, you, La Martineau, who got the judges to condemn God and me, here's one stone, and two, and three! Yes, wait a moment, you shall have a stone for every one of those five and twenty francs!'

The scandal was tremendous; two women were struck, and the rural guard, who had now come up, at once began to scribble an official report. Amidst the shouting and hooting Abbé Cognasse suddenly recovered his senses. Like some deity threatening the world with destruction he made a last fierce gesture, then sprang down his ladder, and disappeared like a Jack into his box. He had just set another fine lawsuit on his shoulders, which bent already beneath a pile of citations.

On the following Thursday Marc repaired to Maillebois, and a fancy which had been haunting him for some time past was then suddenly changed into certainty. While crossing the little Place des Capucins, his attention was attracted by a wretched-looking man, who stood in front of the Brothers' school gazing fixedly at the dilapidated walls. And Marc immediately recognised this man to be the one whom he had perceived with Polydor, in the avenue leading to the railway station, a month previously. This time he had no cause for hesitation. He was able to examine the man at his ease, in the broad sunlight, and he saw that he was, indeed, Brother Gorgias—Gorgias, in old and greasy clothing, with hollow cheeks and bent limbs, but still easily recognisable by the large, fierce beak which jutted out from between his projecting cheek-bones. Thus Delbos had not been mistaken; Gorgias had really returned, and, doubtless, had been prowling about the region for a good many months already.

The Ignorantine, amid the reverie into which he had sunk as he stood on that sleepy and almost invariably deserted little square, must have become conscious of the scrutinising gaze which was being directed upon him. He slowly turned round, and his eyes then met those of the man who stood only a few steps away. And he, on his side, assuredly recognised Marc. Instead, however, of evincing any alarm, instead of taking to his heels as he had done on the first occasion, he lingered there, and his old sneer, that involuntary twitching of the lips which disclosed some of his wolfish teeth in a manner suggesting both contempt and cruelty, appeared upon his face. Then, pointing to the tumble-down walls of the Brothers' school, he said quietly: 'That sight must please you every time you pass this way—eh,

Monsieur Froment?... It angers me; I'd like to set fire to the shanty, and burn the last of those cowards in it!'

Then, as Marc shuddered without replying, thunderstruck as he was by the bandit's audacity in addressing him, Gorgias again grinned in his silent, evil way, and added: 'Are you astonished that I should confess myself to you? You, no doubt, were my worst enemy. But, after all, why should I bear you malice? You owed me nothing, you were fighting for your own opinions.... The men I hate and whom I mean to pursue until my last breath are my superiors, my brothers in Jesus Christ, all those whose duty it was to cover and save me, but who flung me into the streets, hoping I should die of shame and starvation.... I myself, it may be allowed, am but a poor and erring creature, but it was God whom those wretched cowards betrayed and sold, for it is their fault, the fault of their imbecile weakness if the Church is now near to defeat, and if that poor school yonder is already falling to pieces.... Ah! when one remembers what a position it held in my time! We were the victors then; we had reduced your secular schools to next to nothing. But now they are triumphing, and will soon be the only ones left. The thought of it fills me with regret and anger!'

Then, as two old women crossed the square and a Capuchin came out of the neighbouring chapel, Gorgias, after glancing anxiously about him, added swiftly in an undertone: 'Listen to me, Monsieur Froment; for a long time past I have wished to have a chat with you. If you are willing I will call on you at Jonville some day, after nightfall.'

Then he hurried off, disappearing before Marc could say a word. The schoolmaster, who was quite upset by that meeting, spoke of it to nobody excepting his wife, who felt alarmed when she heard of it. They agreed that they would not admit that man if he should venture to call on them, for the visit he announced might well prove to be some machination of treachery and falsehood. Gorgias had always lied, and he would lie again; so it was absurd to expect from him any useful new fact such as had been sought so long. However, some months elapsed and the other made no sign; in such wise that Marc who, at the outset, had remained watchful with a view of keeping his door shut, gradually grew astonished and impatient. He wondered what might be the things which Gorgias had wished to tell him; and a desire to know them worried him more and more. After all, why should he not receive the scamp? Even if he learnt nothing useful from him, he would have an opportunity of fathoming his nature. And having come to that conclusion, Marc lived on in suspense, waiting for the visit which was so long deferred.

At last, one winter evening, when the rain was pouring in torrents, Brother Gorgias presented himself, clad in an old cloak, streaming with mud and water. As soon as he had rid himself of that rag, Marc showed him into his classroom, which was still warm, for the fire in the faïence stove was only just dying out. A little oil lamp alone cast some light over a portion of that large and silent room around which big shadows had gathered. And Geneviève, trembling slightly with a vague fear of some possible attempt upon her husband, remained listening behind a door.

As for Brother Gorgias, he, without any ado, resumed the conversation interrupted on the Place des Capucins, as if it had taken place that very afternoon.

'You know, Monsieur Froment,' he began, 'the Church is dying because she no longer possesses any priests resolute enough to support her by fire and steel, if need be. Not one of the poor fools, the whimpering clowns of the present day, loves or even knows the real God—He who at once exterminated the nations that dared to disobey Him, and who reigned over the bodies and souls of men like an absolute master, ever armed with resistless thunderbolts.... How can you expect the world to be different from what it is, if the Deity now merely has poltroons and fools to speak in His name?'

Then Gorgias enumerated his superiors, his brothers in Christ, as he called them, one by one, and a perfect massacre ensued. Monseigneur Bergerot, who had lately died at the advanced age of eighty-seven, had never been aught than a poor, timid, incoherent creature, lacking the necessary courage to secede from Rome and establish that famous liberal and rationalist Church of France which he had dreamt of, and which would have been little else than a new Protestant sect. Those lettered Bishops gifted with inquiring minds, but destitute of all sturdiness of faith, suffered the incredulous masses to desert the altars instead of flagellating them mercilessly with the dread of hell. But Gorgias's most intense hatred was directed against Abbé Quandieu, who still survived though his eightieth year was past. For the Ignorantine the ex-priest of St. Martin's was a perjurer, an apostate, a bad priest who had spat upon his own religion by openly upholding God's enemies at the time of the Simon case. Moreover, he had abandoned his ministry, and gone to dwell in a little house in a lonely neighbourhood, impudently saying that he was disgusted with the base superstition of the last believers, and carrying his audacity so far as to pretend that the monks, whom he called the traders of the Temple, were demolishers who unconsciously hastened the downfall of the Church. But if there was a demolisher it was he himself, for his desertion had served as an argument to the enemies of Catholicism. Surely indeed it was an abominable example that he had set—forswearing all his past life, breaking his vows, and preferring a sleek and shameful old age to martyrdom. As for that big, lean, stern Abbé Coquart, his successor at St. Martin's, however imposing the newcomer might look he was in reality only a fool.

Marc had, for a while, listened in silence, determined to offer no interruption. But his feelings rebelled when he heard Gorgias's violent attack upon Abbé Quandieu. 'You do not know that priest,' he said quietly. 'Your judgment is that of an enemy, blinded by spite.... As a matter of fact, Abbé Quandieu was the only priest of this region who, at the outset, understood what frightful harm the Church would do herself by openly and passionately defying truth and justice. She claims to represent a Deity of certainty and equity, kindness and innocence; she was founded to exalt the suffering and the meek, and yet, all at once, in order to retain temporal authority, she makes common cause with oppressors and liars and forgers! It was certain that the consequences would be terrible for her as soon as Simon's innocence should become manifest. Such conduct was suicide on the Church's part. With her own hands she prepared her condemnation, showing the world that she was no longer the abode of the true and the just, of everlasting purity and goodness! And her expiation is only just beginning; she will slowly die of that denial of justice which she took upon herself and which has become a devouring sore.... Abbé Quandieu foresaw it and said it. It is not true that he fled from the Church in any spirit of cowardice; he quitted his ministry bleeding and weeping, and it is in grief that he is ending a life of misery and bitterness.'

By a rough gesture Gorgias signified that he did not intend to argue. With his glowing eyes gazing far away into the galling memories of his personal experiences, he scarcely listened to Marc, impatient as he was to continue his own rageful diatribe.

'Good, good, I say what I think,' he resumed, 'but I don't prevent you from thinking whatever you please.... There are, at all events, other imbeciles and cowards whom you won't defend, for instance, that rascal Father Théodose, the mirror of the devotees, the thieving cashier of heaven!'

Thereupon Gorgias assailed the superior of the Capuchins with murderous fury. He did not blame the worship of St. Antony of Padua. On the contrary he praised it; he set all his hopes in miracles, he would have liked to have seen the whole world bringing money to the shrine of the Saint in order that the latter might persuade the Deity to hurl His thunderbolts upon the cities of sin. But Father Théodose was a mere conscienceless mountebank, who amassed money for himself alone, and gave no assistance whatever to the afflicted servants of God. Though hundreds of thousands of francs had formerly overflowed from his collection boxes, he had not devoted even an occasional five-franc piece to render life a little less hard than it was to the poor Brothers of the Christian Doctrine, his neighbours. And now that the gifts he received were dwindling year by year his avarice was even greater. He had refused the smallest alms to him, Brother Gorgias, at a time when he was in the most desperate circumstances, when, indeed, a ten-franc piece might have saved his life.

They all abandoned him, yes, all—not only that lecherous money-mongering Father Théodose, but even the other, the great chief, the great culprit, who was as big a fool as he was a rascal. Then Gorgias blurted out the name of Father Crabot which had been burning his lips. Ah! Father Crabot, Father Crabot, he had worshipped him in former times, he had served him on his knees in respectful silence, ready to carry his devotion to the point of crime. He had then regarded him as an all-powerful, able, and valiant master, favoured by Jesus, who had promised him eternal victory in this world. By Father Crabot's side he, Gorgias, had thought himself protected from the wicked, assured of success in every enterprise, even the most dangerous. And yet that venerated master to whom he had dedicated his life, that glorious Father Crabot, now denied him and left him without shelter and without a crust. He did worse indeed; he cast him upon the waters as if he were a troublesome accomplice, whose disappearance was desired. Besides, had he not always displayed the most monstrous egotism? Had he not previously sacrificed poor Father Philibin, who had lately died in the Italian convent where he had lingered, virtually dead, for many years already? Father Philibin had been a hero, a victim, who had invariably obeyed his superior, who had carried devotion so far as to take upon his shoulders all the punishment for the deeds which had been commanded of him and which he had done in silence. Yet another victim was that hallucinated Brother Fulgence, a perfect nincompoop with his excitable sparrow's brain, but who, none the less, had not deserved to be swept away into the nothingness in which, somewhere or other, he was dying. What good purpose had been served by all that villainy and ingratitude? Had it not been as stupid as it was cruel on Father Crabot's part to abandon in that fashion all his old friends, all the instruments of his fortune? Had not his own position been shaken by his conduct in allowing the others to be struck down? And had he never thought that one of them might at last grow weary of it all, and rise up and cast terrible truths in his face?

'Beneath all Crabot's grand manners,' cried Brother Gorgias excitedly, 'beneath all his reputation for cleverness and diplomatic skill, there is rank stupidity. He must be quite a fool to treat me in the way he does. But let him take care, let him take care, or else one of these days, before long, I shall speak out!'

At this, Marc, who had been listening with passionate interest, made an effort to hasten the other's revelations: 'Speak out? What have you to say then?' he inquired.

'Nothing, nothing, there are only some matters between him and me—I shall tell them to God alone, in a confession.' Then, reverting to his bitter catalogue of accusations, Gorgias exclaimed: 'And, to finish, there's that Brother Joachim, whom they have set at the head of our school at Maillebois in Brother Fulgence's place. Joachim is another of Father Crabot's creatures, a hypocrite, chosen on account of his supposed skill and artfulness—one who imagines himself to be a great man because he does not pull the ears of the little vermin entrusted to him. You know the result—the school will soon have to be closed for lack of pupils! If the wretched offspring of men are to grow up fairly well, they must be trained by kicks and blows, as God requires.... And—if you want my opinion—there is only one priest imbued with the right spirit in the whole region, and that is your Abbé Cognasse. He, too, went to seek advice at Valmarie, and they nearly rotted him as they rotted the others, by advising him to be supple and crafty. But he fortunately regained possession of himself; it is with stones that he now pursues the enemies of the Church! That is the right course for the real saints to follow, that is the way in which God, when He chooses to interfere, will end by reconquering the world!'

Thus speaking, Gorgias raised his clenched fists and brandished them wildly, vehemently, in that usually quiet classroom where the little lamp shed but a faint glimmer of light. Then, for a moment, came deep silence, amid which one only heard the pouring rain pattering on the window-panes.

'Well, at all events,' said Marc with a touch of irony, 'God seems to have forsaken and sacrificed you even as your superiors have done.'

Brother Gorgias glanced at his wretched clothes and emaciated hands which testified to his sufferings. 'It is true,' he answered, 'God has chastised me severely for my transgressions and for those of others. I bow to His will, He is working my salvation. But I do not forget, I do not forgive the others for having aggravated my misery. Ah, the bandits! Have they not condemned me to the most frightful existence ever since they compelled me to quit Maillebois? It is in misery that I have had to come back here to endeavour to wring from them the crust of bread which is my due!'

He was unwilling to say more on that subject, but his tragic story could be well divined by the shudder that came over him—the shudder of a wild beast driven from the woods by hunger. The Order, no doubt, had sent him from community to community, the poorest, the most obscure, until at last it had finally cast him out altogether as being by far too compromising. And then he had quitted his gown and rolled along the roads, carrying with him the stigma attaching to a disfrocked cleric. One would never know through what distant lands he had roamed, what a life of privation and chance he had led, what unacknowledgeable adventures he had met with, what shameful vices he had indulged in: one could only read a little of all that on the tanned skin of his eager face, in the depths of his eyes which glowed with suffering and hatred. The greater part of his resources must certainly have come from his former confederates, who had wished to purchase his silence and keep him at a distance. Every now and again, when he had written letter upon letter, when he had furiously threatened crushing revelations, some small sum had been sent to him, and then for a few months he had been able to prolong the wretched life he led as a waif whom all rejected.

But at last a time had come when he had no longer received any answer to his applications, when his letters and his threats had remained without any effect; for his former superiors had grown weary of his voracious demands, and regarded him, perhaps, as being no longer dangerous after the lapse of so many years. He himself was intelligent enough to understand that his confessions could no longer have any very serious consequences for his accomplices, but might even deprive him of his last chance of extracting money from them. Nevertheless he had resolved to return and prowl around Maillebois. He knew the Code, he was aware that the law of limitation covered him. And thus for long months he had been living, in some dark nook, on the five-franc pieces which he wrung from the fears of Simon's accusers, who still trembled at the thought of their shameful victory at Rozan. Yet they must again have been growing weary of his persecution, for his bitterness was too great; he would never have heaped so many insults upon them if they had let him dip his hands in their purses, the previous day, by way of once more purchasing his silence.

Marc readily understood the position. Brother Gorgias only sprang out of the suspicious darkness in which he concealed himself when he had spent his money in crapulous debauchery. And if he had come to Jonville that winter night, in the pouring rain, it was assuredly because his pockets were empty and because he expected to derive some profit from that visit. But what profit could it be? What motive lurked beneath his long and furious denunciation of the men of whom, according to his own account, he had only been a docile instrument?

'So you are living at Maillebois?' inquired Marc, whose curiosity was fully awakened.

'No, no, not at Maillebois.... I live where I can.'

'But I thought I had already seen you there before meeting you on the Place des Capucins.... You were with one of your former pupils—Polydor, I fancy.'

A faint smile appeared on Brother Gorgias's ravaged face. 'Polydor,' said he, 'yes, yes, I was always very fond of him. He was a pious and discreet lad. Like myself he has suffered from the maliciousness of men. He has been accused of all sorts of crimes, cast out unjustly by people who did not understand his nature. And I was glad to meet him when I returned here; we set our wretchedness together, and consoled each other, abandoning ourselves to the divine arms of our Lord.... But Polydor is young, and he will end by treating me as the others have done. For a month past I have been looking for him: he has disappeared. Ah! everything is going wrong, there must be an end to it all!'

A raucous sigh escaped him, and Marc shuddered, for Gorgias's manner and tone as he referred to Polydor afforded a glimpse of yet another hell. But there was no time for reflection. Drawing nearer to the schoolmaster the disfrocked brother resumed: 'Now, listen to me, Monsieur Froment; I have had enough of it, I have come to tell you everything.... Yes, if you will promise to listen to me as a priest would listen, I will tell you the truth, the real truth. You are the only man to whom I can make such a confession without doing violence to my dignity or pride, for you alone have always been a disinterested and loyal enemy.... So receive my confession, on the one understanding that you will keep it secret until I authorise you to divulge it.'

But Marc hastily interrupted him: 'No, no, I will not enter into such a compact. I have done nothing to provoke any revelations on your part; you have come here of your own accord, and you say what you please. Should you really place the truth in my hands, I mean to remain at liberty to make use of it according as my conscience may bid me.'

Brother Gorgias scarcely hesitated. 'Well, let it be so; it is in your conscience that I will confide,' said he.

Nevertheless he did not immediately speak out. Silence fell once more. The rain was still streaming down the window panes, and gusts of wind howled along the deserted streets, while the flame of the little lamp began to flare amid the vague shadows which hovered about the quiet room. Marc, gradually growing uncomfortable, suffering from all the abominable memories which that man's presence aroused, glanced anxiously at the door behind which Geneviève must have remained. Had she heard what had been said? If so how uncomfortable must the stirring up of all that old mud have made her feel also!

At last, after long remaining silent as if to impart yet more solemnity to his confession, Brother Gorgias raised his hand towards the ceiling in a dramatic manner, and after a fresh interval said slowly, in a rough voice: 'It is true, I confess it before God, I entered little Zéphirin's room on the night of the crime!'

At this, although Marc awaited the promised confession with a good deal of scepticism, expecting to hear merely some more falsehoods, he was unable to overcome a great shudder, a feeling of horror, which made him spring to his feet. But Gorgias quietly motioned him to his chair again.

'I entered the room,' said he, 'or rather I leant from outside on the window-bar at about twenty minutes past ten o'clock, before the crime. And that is what I wished to tell you, in order to relieve my conscience.... On leaving the Capuchin Chapel that night I undertook to escort little Polydor to the cottage of his father, the road-mender, on the way to Jonville, for fear of any mishap befalling the lad. We left the chapel at ten o'clock, and if I took ten minutes to escort Polydor home and ten minutes to return, it must, you see, have been about twenty minutes past ten when I again passed before the school. As I crossed the little deserted square I was surprised to see Zéphirin's window lighted up and wide open. I drew near, and I saw the dear child in his nightdress, setting out some religious prints, which some of his companions at the first Communion had given him. And I scolded him for not having closed his window, for the first passer-by might easily have sprung into his room. But he laughed in his pretty way, and complained of feeling very hot. It was, as you must remember, a close and stormy night.... Well, I was making him promise that he would do as I told him, and go to bed as soon as possible, when, among the religious pictures set out on his table, I saw a copy-slip which had come from my class, and which was stamped and initialled by me. It made me angry to see it there, and I reminded Zéphirin that the boys were forbidden to take away anything belonging to the school. He turned very red, and tried to excuse himself, saying that he had taken the slip home in order to finish an exercise. And he asked me to leave the slip with him, promising to bring it back the next morning, and restore it to me.... Then he closed his window, and I went off. That is the truth, the whole truth, I swear it before God!'

Marc, who had how recovered his calmness, gazed at Gorgias fixedly, endeavouring to conceal his impressions. 'You are quite sure that the boy shut his window when you went away?' he asked.

'He shut it, and I heard him putting up the shutter-bar.'

'Then you still assert that Simon was guilty, for nobody could have got in from outside; and you hold that Simon, after the crime, opened the shutters again in order to cast suspicion on some unknown prowler?'

'Yes, it is still my opinion that Simon was the culprit. But there is also this chance, that Zéphirin, oppressed by the heat, may have opened the window again after I had gone.'

Marc was not deceived by that supposition, which was offered him as a guide that might lead to a new fact. He even shrugged his shoulders, feeling that as Gorgias still accused another of his crime, his pretended confession had little value. At the same time, however, that medley of fact and fiction cast just a little more light on the affair, and this Marc desired to establish.

'Why did you not relate at the Assizes what you have now stated?' he inquired. 'A great act of injustice might then have been avoided.'

'Why I did not relate it?' Gorgias replied. 'Why, because I should have compromised myself to no good purpose! My own innocence would have been doubted, and besides, I was then already convinced of Simon's guilt even as I am now; and thus my silence was quite natural.... Moreover, I repeat it, I had seen the copy-slip lying on the table.'

'Yes, only you now admit that it came from your school and that you had stamped and initialled it yourself. You did not always say that, remember.'

'Oh! those fools, Father Crabot and the others, imposed a ridiculous story on me; and to prop up their senseless theory with the help of their grotesque experts they afterwards invented the still more foolish idea of a forged stamp.... For my part, I at once desired to admit the authenticity of the copy-slip, which was self-evident. But I had to bow to their authority, accept their ridiculous inventions, under penalty of being abandoned and sacrificed.... You saw how furious they became before the trial at Rozan, when I ended by acknowledging that the paraph was mine. They wanted to save that unfortunate Philibin; they fancied they were clever enough to spare the Church even the shadow of a suspicion, and for that very reason they do not even now forgive me for having ceased to repeat their lies!'

Then Marc, noticing that Gorgias was gradually becoming exasperated, said, as if thinking aloud and by way of spurring him on: 'All the same, it is very strange that the copy-slip should have been on the child's table.'

'Strange! why? It often happened that one of the boys took a slip away with him. Little Victor Milhomme had taken one, and it was that very circumstance that made you suspect the truth as to the origin of the slip.... But do you still accuse me of being the murderer? Do you still believe that I walked about with that slip in my pocket? Come, is it reasonable—eh?'

Gorgias spoke with such jeering, aggressive violence, his lips twitching the while with that rictus which disclosed his wolfish teeth, that Marc slightly lost countenance. In spite of his conviction of the brother's guilt, that slip, which had come nobody knew whence, had always seemed to him a very obscure feature of the affair. Even as the Ignorantine constantly repeated, it was scarcely likely that he had carried the paper in his pocket that evening on quitting the ceremony at the Capuchin Chapel. Whence had it come then? How was it that Gorgias had found it mingled with a copy of *Le Petit Beaumontais*? Marc felt that if he had been able to penetrate that mystery the whole affair would have been perfectly clear. To conceal his perplexity he tried an argument: 'It wasn't necessary for you to have the slip in your pocket,' said he, 'for you have said that you saw it lying on the table.'

But Brother Gorgias had now risen, either yielding to his usual vehemence or playing some comedy in order to end the interview, which was not taking the course he desired. Black and bent, he walked up and down the shadowy room, gesticulating wildly.

'On the table, yes, of course I saw it on the table! If I say that, it is because I have nothing to fear from such an admission. You suppose me to be guilty, but in that case do you imagine I should give you a weapon by telling you where I took the slip!... We say it was on the table, eh? So it would follow that I took it up, and took a newspaper also out of my pocket, and crumpled it up with the slip, in order to turn both into a gag. What an operation—eh?—at such a moment, how logical and simple it would have been!... But no, no! If the newspaper was in my pocket the slip must have been there also. Prove that it was; for otherwise you have nothing substantial and decisive to go upon. And it wasn't in my pocket, for I saw it on the table, I swear it again before God!'

Wildly, savagely, he drew near to Marc and cast in his face those words in which one detected a kind of audacious provocation, compounded of scraps of truth, impudently set forth in the shape of suppositions, falsehoods that barely masked the frightful scene which he must have lived afresh with a frightful, demoniacal delight.

But Marc, cast into disturbing perplexity, feeling that he would learn nothing useful from his visitor, had also decided to end the interview.

'Listen,' said he, 'why should I believe you? You come here and you tell me a tale which is the third version you have given of the affair.... At the outset you agreed with the prosecution; the slip, you said, belonged to the secular school; you did not initial it; it was Simon who had done so in order to cast his crime on you. Then, on the discovery of the stamped corner torn off by Father Philibin, you felt it impossible to shelter yourself any longer behind the stupid report of the experts; you admitted that the initialling was your work, and that the slip had come from you. At present, with what motive I do not know, you make a fresh confession to me; you assert that you saw little Zéphirin in his room a few minutes before the crime, that the copy-slip was then lying on his table, that you scolded him, and that he closed his shutters.... Well, think it over; there is no reason why I should regard this version as final. I shall wait to hear the plain truth, if indeed it ever pleases you to tell it.'

Pausing in his stormy perambulations, Brother Gorgias drew up his gaunt and tragic figure. His eyes were blazing, an evil laugh distorted his face once more. For a moment he remained silent. Then in a jeering way he said: 'As you choose, Monsieur Froment! I came here in a friendly spirit to give you some particulars about the affair, which still interests you as you have not renounced the hope of getting Simon rehabilitated. You can make use of those particulars; I authorise you to make them known. And I ask you for no thanks, for I no longer expect any gratitude from men.'

Then he wrapped himself in his ragged cloak, and went off as he had come, opening the doors himself, and giving never a glance behind. Outside the icy rain was coming down in furious squalls, the wind filled the street with its howls, and Gorgias vanished like a ghost into the depths of the lugubrious darkness.

Geneviève had now opened the door behind which she had remained listening. Stupefied by all she had heard she let her arms drop, and for a moment remained gazing at Marc, who likewise stood there motionless, at a loss whether to laugh or to feel angry.

'He is mad, my friend,' said Geneviève. 'If I had been in your place I should not have had the patience to listen to him so long; he lies as he has always lied!' Then, as Marc seemed inclined to take things gaily, she continued: 'No, no, it is not at all amusing. The revival of all those horrid things has made me feel quite ill and anxious also, for I do not understand what can have been his purpose in coming here. Why did he make that pretended confession? Why did he select you to hear it?'

'Oh! I think I know, my dear,' Marc answered. 'In all probability Father Crabot and the others no longer give him a copper, that is, apart from some petty monthly allowance which they may have arranged to make him. And as the rascal has a huge appetite he tries to terrify them from time to time, in order to extract some big sum from them. I have had information; they have done their utmost to induce him to leave the region. Twice already, by filling his pockets they have prevailed on him to do so; but as soon as his pockets were empty he came back. They dare not employ the police in the affair, otherwise the gendarmes would have rid them of him long ago. And so, once again, as they have refused to let him have more money, he wishes to give them a good fright by threatening to tell me everything. And he has told me just a little truth mixed with a great deal of falsehood, in the hope that I may speak of it, and that the others in their fright may pay him well to prevent him from telling me all the rest.'

This logical explanation restored the calmness of Geneviève, who merely added: 'The rest—the full, plain truth—he will never tell it!'

'Who knows?' Marc retorted. 'His craving for money is great, but there is yet more hatred in his heart. And he is courageous; he would willingly risk his skin to revenge himself on those old accomplices who have cowardly forsaken him. Moreover, in spite of all his crimes, he really belongs to his Deity of extermination; he glows with a sombre, devouring faith, which would prompt him to martyrdom if he only thought that he might thereby win salvation and cast his enemies into the torments of hell.'

'Shall you try to make any use of what he told you?' Geneviève inquired.

'No, I think not. I shall talk it over with Delbos; but he, I know, has resolved that he will only move when he has a certainty to act upon.... Ah! poor Simon, I despair of ever seeing him rehabilitated; I have become so old!'

All at once, however, the new fact, awaited for so many years, became manifest, and Marc then beheld the realisation of the most ardent desire of his life. Delbos, who placed no faith in any help from Brother Gorgias, had set all his hopes on the Rozan medical man, that Dr. Beauchamp, a juror at the second trial, to whom Judge Gragnon was said to have made his second illegal communication, and who was reported to be tortured by remorse. This scent Delbos followed with infinite patience, having a watch kept upon the doctor, who preserved silence in compliance with the entreaties of his wife, a very pious and also sickly woman, whose death would probably have been hastened by any scandal. All at once indeed she died, and Delbos then no longer doubted the success of his enterprise. It took him another six months to perfect his arrangements; he managed to enter into direct relations with Beauchamp, whom he found all anxiety and indecision, assailed by a variety of scruples. But at last the doctor made up his mind to hand the advocate a signed statement in which he related how one day a friend, acting on behalf of Gragnon, had shown him the pretended confession which a workman, dying at the Beaumont hospital, was said to have made to one of the sisters—a confession in which this man acknowledged that he had engraved a false stamp for Simon, the Maillebois schoolmaster. And Beauchamp added that this secret communication alone had convinced him of the guilt of Simon, whom previously he had been disposed to acquit for lack of all serious proof.

Having secured this decisive statement Delbos did not act precipitately. He waited a little longer. He gathered together other documents, which showed that Gragnon had communicated his extravagant forgery to other jurors, men of the most amazing credulity. Equally extraordinary was it to find that the ex-presiding judge had dared to repeat the trick of Beaumont, carrying a gross forgery in his pocket, circulating it secretly through Rozan, exploiting human imbecility with the most sovereign contempt. And twice had the trick succeeded, Gragnon on the second occasion saving himself from the galleys by sheer criminal audacity. He was now beyond the reach of punishment, for he had lately died, perishing miserably, quite withered away, his features furrowed, it seemed, by invisible claws. And it was certainly his death which had induced Dr. Beauchamp to speak out.

Marc and David had long thought that the Simon affair would be quite settled when the personages compromised in it should have disappeared. At present ex-investigating Magistrate Daix was also dead, while the former Procureur de la République, Raoul de La Bissonnière, had lately been retired with the grant of a Commandership of the Legion of Honour. Then Counsellor Guybaraud, who had presided at the Assizes at Rozan, having been stricken with hemiplegia, was passing away between his confessor and a servant-mistress; whereas Pacard, the ex-demagogue who in spite of a nasty story of cheating at cards had managed to become a public prosecutor, had quitted the magistracy to take up somewhat mysterious duties at Rome as legal adviser to some of the congregations. Again, at Beaumont there were great changes in the political, administrative, clerical, and teaching worlds. Other men had succeeded Lemarrois, Marcilly, Hennebise, Bergerot, Forbes, and Mauraisin. Of the direct accomplices in the crime, Father Philibin had died far away, Brother Fulgence had disappeared, being also dead perhaps, in such wise that there only remained Father Crabot, the great chief. But even he had withdrawn from among the living, cloistered, it was alleged, in some lonely cell, where he was spending his last years in great penitence.

And thus there was quite a new social atmosphere; politics had altogether changed, men's passions were no longer the same when Delbos, having at last collected the weapons he desired, brought the affair forward once more with masterly energy. Of recent years he had risen to a position of influence in the Chamber of Deputies, so he took his documents straight to the Minister of Justice and speedily prevailed on him to lay the new fact before the Court of Cassation. It is true that a debate on the subject ensued the very next day, but the Minister contented himself with stating that the matter was purely and simply a legal one, and that the Government could not allow it to be turned once more into a political question. And then, amid the indifference with which this old Simon affair was now regarded, a vote of confidence in the Government was passed by a considerable majority. As for the Court of Cassation, which still smarted from the smack it had received at Rozan, it tried the case with extraordinary despatch, purely and simply annulling the Rozan verdict without sending Simon before any other tribunal. It was all, so to say, a mere formality; in three phrases everything was effaced, and justice was done at last.

Thus, then, in all simplicity, the innocence of Simon was recognised and proclaimed amid the pure glow of truth triumphant after so many years of falsehood and of crime.

CHAPTER III

On the morrow of the court's judgment there came an extraordinary revival of emotion at Maillebois. There was no surprise, for those who now believed in Simon's innocence were very numerous; but the material fact of that decisive legal rehabilitation upset everybody. And the same thought came to men of the most varied views. They approached one another, and they said:

'What! can no possible reparation be offered to that unfortunate man who suffered so dreadfully? Doubtless neither money nor honours of any kind could indemnify him for his horrible martyrdom. But when a whole people has been guilty of such an abominable error, when it has turned a fellow-being into such a pitiable, suffering creature, it would be good that it should acknowledge its fault, and confer some triumph on that man by a great act of frankness, in which truth and justice would find recognition.'

From that moment, indeed, the idea that reparation was necessary gained ground, spreading by degrees through the entire region. One circumstance touched every heart. While the Court of Cassation was examining the documents respecting the illegal communication made at Rozan, old Lehmann, the tailor, who had reached his ninetieth year, lay dying in that wretched house of the Rue du Trou which had been saddened by so many tears and so much mourning. His daughter Rachel had hastened from her Pyrenean retreat in order that she might be beside him at the last hour. But every morning, by some effort of will, the old man seemed to revive; being unwilling to die, said he, so long as justice should not have been done to the honour of his son-in-law and his grandchildren. And, indeed, it was only on the night of the day when the news of the acquittal reached him that he at last expired, radiant with supreme joy.

After the funeral Rachel immediately rejoined Simon and David in their solitude, where they intended to remain for another four or five years, when perhaps they might sell their marble quarry and liquidate their little fortune. And it so happened that the old house of the Rue du Trou was now demolished, a happy inspiration coming to the Municipal Council of Maillebois to purify that sordid district of the town by carrying a broad thoroughfare through it, and laying out a small recreation-ground for the working-class children. Sarah, whose husband Sébastien had now been appointed head-master of one of the Beaumont schools, had sold the tailoring business to a Madame Savin, a relative of those Savins who in former times had pelted her brother Joseph and herself with stones; and thus no trace remained of the spot where the Simon family had wept so bitterly in the distant days, when each letter arriving from the innocent prisoner in the penal settlement yonder had brought them fresh torture. Trees now grew there in the sunshine, flowers shed their perfume beside the lawns, and it seemed as if it were from that health-bringing spot that spread the covert remorse of Maillebois, its desire to repair the frightful iniquity of the past.

Nevertheless, things slumbered for a long time yet. A period of four years went by, during which only individual suggestions were made, no general agreement being arrived at. But generation was following generation; after the children had come the grandchildren, and then the great-grandchildren of those who had persecuted Simon, in such wise that quite a new population ended by dwelling in Maillebois. Yet it was necessary for the great evolution towards other social conditions to be entirely accomplished, in order that the seed which had been sown should yield a harvest of citizens freed from error and falsehood, to whom one might look for a great manifestation of equity.

Meantime life continued, and the valiant workers whose task was completed made way for their children. Marc and Geneviève, now nearly seventy years old, retired, and the Jonville schools were entrusted to their son Clément and his wife Charlotte, Hortense Savin's daughter, who, like himself, had adopted the teaching profession. Mignot, on his side, had quitted Le Moreux and retired to Jonville, in order to be near Marc and Geneviève, who dwelt in a small house near their old school. Thus the village held quite a little colony of the first participators in the great enterprise, for Salvan and Mademoiselle Mazeline were still alive, enjoying a smiling and kindly old age. Then, at Maillebois, the boys' school was in the hands of Joseph, and the girls' school in those of his wife Louise. He was now forty-four, she two years younger; and they had a big son, François, who, in his twenty-second year, had married his cousin Thérèse, the daughter of Sébastien and Sarah, by whom he had a beautiful baby-girl named Rose, now barely a twelvemonth old. Joseph and Louise were bent on never quitting Maillebois, and they gently chaffed Sébastien and Sarah respecting the honours which awaited them; for there was now a question of appointing Sébastien to the directorship of the Training College where Salvan had worked so well. As for François and Thérèse, who by hereditary vocation had also adopted the scholastic profession, they now dwelt at Dherbecourt, where both had become assistant teachers. And what a swarming of the sowers of truth there was on certain Sundays when the whole family assembled at Jonville round the grandparents, Marc and Geneviève! And what fine, bright health was brought from Beaumont by Sébastien and Sarah, from Maillebois by Joseph and Louise, from Dherbecourt by François and Thérèse, who came carrying their little Rose; while at Jonville they were met by Clément and Charlotte, who also had a daughter, Lucienne, now a big girl, nearly seven years of age! And, again, what a table had to be laid for that gathering of the four generations, particularly when their good friends Salvan, Mignot, and Mademoiselle Mazeline were willing to join them to drink to the defeat of Ignorance, the parent of every evil and every form of servitude!

The times of human liberation, which had been so long in coming, which had been awaited so feverishly, were now being brought to pass by sudden evolutions. A terrible blow had been dealt to the Church, for the last Legislature had voted the complete separation of Church and State, [1] and the millions formerly given to the priests, who had employed them to perpetuate among the people both hatred of the Republic and such abasement as was suited to a flock kept merely to be sheared, would now be better employed in doubling the salaries of the elementary schoolmasters. Thus the situation was entirely changed: the schoolmaster ceased to be the poor devil, the ill-paid varlet, whom the peasant regarded with so much contempt when he thought of the well-paid priest, who waxed fat on surplice fees and the presents of the devout. The priest ceased to be a functionary, drawing pay from the State revenue, supported both by the prefect and by the bishop; and thus he lost the respect of the country-folk. They no longer feared him; he was but a kind of chance sacristan, dependent on a few remaining believers, who from time to time paid him for a Mass. Again, the churches ceased to be State institutions, and became theatres run on commercial lines, subsisting on the payments made by the spectators, the last admirers of the ceremonies performed in them. It was certain, too, that before long many would have to close their doors, business already being so bad with some that they were threatened with bankruptcy. And nothing could be more typical than the position of that terrible Abbé Cognasse, whose outbursts of passion had so long upset Le Moreux and Jonville. His numerous lawsuits had remained famous; one could no longer count the number of times he had been fined for pulling boys' ears, kicking women, and flinging stones from his garden wall upon those passers who declined to make the sign of the Cross. Nevertheless, he had retained his office amid all the worries brought upon him by the citations he received, for he was virtually irremovable and exercised a paid State function. When, however, in consequence of the separation of Church and State, he suddenly became merely the representative of an opinion, a belief, when he ceased to receive

State pay to impose that belief on others, he lapsed into such nothingness that people no longer bowed to him. In a few months' time he found himself almost alone in his church with his old servant Palmyre, for, however much the latter might pull the bell-rope with her shrivelled arms, only some five or six women still came to Mass. A little later there were but three, and finally only one came. She, fortunately, persevered, and the Abbé was pleased to be able to celebrate the offices in her presence, for he feared lest he should have the same deplorable experience at Jonville as he had encountered at Le Moreux. During a period of three months he had gone every Sunday to the latter village in order to say Mass without even being able to get a child as server, so that he had been obliged to take his little clerk with him from Jonville. And during those three months nobody had come to worship; he had officiated in solitude in the dank, dark, empty church. Naturally, he had ended by no longer returning thither, and at present the closed church was rotting away and falling into ruins. When, indeed, one of the functions of social life disappears, the building and the man associated with it become useless and likewise disappear. And in spite of the violent demeanour which Abbé Cognasse still preserved, his great dread was that he might see his last parishioner forsake him and his church closed, crumbling away amidst an invading growth of brambles.

> [1] It will be understood that in the above passage M. Zola anticipates events; but it may be remarked that the separation of Church and State in France within a few years has never appeared more likely than it does now (1902-3).—*Trans.*

At Maillebois the separation of Church and State had dealt a last blow to the once prosperous School of the Christian Brothers. Victorious over the secular school at the time of the Simon case, it had fallen into increasing disfavour as the truth had gradually become manifest. But with true clerical obstinacy it had been kept in existence even when only four and five pupils could be recruited for it; and the new laws and the dispersion of the community had been needed to close its doors. The Church was now driven from the national educational service. Henceforth to the sixteen hundred thousand children whom year by year the Congregations had poisoned, a system of purely secular instruction was to be applied. And the reform had spread from the primary to the secondary establishments. Even the celebrated College of Valmarie, already weakened by the expulsion of the Jesuits, was stricken unto death by the great work of renovation which was in progress. The principle of integral and gratuitous instruction for all citizens was beginning to prevail. Why should there be two Frances? Why should there be a lower class doomed to ignorance, and an upper class alone endowed with instruction and culture? Was not this nonsense? Was it not a fault, a danger in a democracy, all of whose children should be called upon to increase the nation's sum of intelligence and strength? In the near future all the children of France, united in a bond of brotherliness, would begin their education in the primary schools, and would thence pass into the secondary and the superior schools, according to their aptitudes, their choice, and their tastes. This was an urgent reform, a great work of salvation and glory, the necessity of which was plainly indicated by the great contemporary social movement, that downfall of the exhausted *bourgeoisie* and the irresistible rise of the masses, in whom quivered the energies of to-morrow. Henceforth it was on them one would have to draw; and among them, as in some huge reservoir of accumulated force, one would find the men of sense, truth, and equity, who, in the name of happiness and peace, would build the city of the future. But, as a first step, the bestowal of gratuitous national education on all the children would finish killing off those pretended free and voluntary schools, those hotbeds of clerical infection, where the only work accomplished was a work of servitude and death. And after the Brothers' school of Maillebois, now empty and long since virtually dead, after the College of Valmarie, whose buildings and grounds were shortly to be sold, the last religious communities would soon disappear, together with all their teaching establishments, their factories of divers kinds, and their princely domains, which represented millions of money filched from human imbecility and expended to maintain the human flock in subjection under the slaughterer's knife.

Nevertheless, near the dismal Brothers' school of Maillebois, where the shutters were closed and where spiders spun their webs in the deserted classrooms, the Capuchin community maintained its chapel dedicated to St. Antony, whose painted and gilded statue still stood there erect in a place of honour. But in vain did Father Théodose, now very aged, exert himself to invent some more extraordinary financial devices. The zeal of the masses was exhausted, and only a few old devotees occasionally slipped half-franc pieces into the dusty collection-boxes. It was rumoured, indeed, that the saint had lost his power. He could no longer even find lost things. One day, too, an old woman actually climbed upon a chair in the chapel and slapped the cheeks of his statue because, instead of healing her sick goat, he had allowed the animal to die. Briefly, thanks to public good sense, aroused at last by the acquirement of a little knowledge, one of the basest of superstitions was dying.

Meantime, at the ancient and venerable parish church of St. Martin's, Abbé Coquard, encountering much the same experience as Abbé Cognasse at Jonville, found himself more and more forsaken, in such wise that it seemed as if he would soon officiate in the solitude and darkness of a necropolis. Unlike Cognasse, however, he evinced no violence. Rigid, gloomy, and silent, he seemed to be leading religion to the grave, preserving the while a sombre stubbornness, refusing to concede anything whatever to the impious men of the age. In his distress he more particularly sought refuge in the worship of the Sacred Heart, decorating his church with all the flags which the neighbouring parishes refused to keep—large red, white, and blue flags, on which huge gory hearts were embroidered in silk and gold. One of his altars, too, was covered with other hearts—of metal, porcelain, goffered leather, and painted mill-board. Of all sizes were these, and one might have thought them just plucked from some bosom, for they seemed to be still warm, to palpitate and shed tears of blood, in such wise that the altar looked like some butcher's gory stall. But that gross re-incarnation no longer touched the masses, which had learnt that a people stricken by disaster raises itself afresh by work and reason, and not by penitence at the feet of monstrous idols. As religions grow old and sink into carnal and base idolatries they seem to rot and fritter away in mouldiness. If the Roman Church, however, was thus at the last gasp, it was, as Abbé Quandieu had said, because it had virtually committed suicide on the day when it had become an upholder of iniquity and falsehood. How was it that it had not foreseen that by siding with liars and forgers it must disappear with them, and share the shame of their infamy on the inevitable day when the innocent and the just would triumph in the full sunlight? Its real master was no longer the Jesus of innocence, of gentleness and charity; it had openly denied Him, driven Him from His temple; and all it retained was that heart of flesh, that barbarous fetish with which it hoped to influence the sick nerves of the poor in spirit. Laden with years and bitterness, Abbé Quandieu had lately passed away repeating: 'They have for the second time condemned and crucified the Lord—the Church will die of it.' And dying it was.

Moreover, it was not passing away alone; the aristocratic and *bourgeois* classes, on which it had vainly sought to lean, were collapsing also. All the ancient noble and military forces, even the financial powers, were collapsing, stricken with madness and impotence, since the reorganisation of the conditions of work had been leading to an equitable distribution of the national wealth. Some characteristic incidents which occurred at La Désirade showed what a wretched fate fell on the whilom rich and powerful, whose millions flowed away like water. Hector de Sanglebœuf lost his seat in the Chamber when the electorate, enlightened and moralised by the new schools, at last rid itself of all reactionary and violent representatives. But a greater misfortune was the death of the Marchioness de Boise, that intelligent and broad-minded woman who had so long promoted prosperity and peace at La Désirade. When she was gone the vain and foolish Sanglebœuf went altogether wrong, becoming a gambler, losing huge sums at play, and descending to ignoble amours; with the result that he was one day brought home beaten unmercifully—so battered, indeed, that three days later he died; no complaint, however, being lodged with the authorities, for fear of all the mud which would soil his memory if the real facts of his death were brought to light.

His wife, the once beautiful and indolent Léa, the pious and ever sleepy Marie of later times, then remained alone amid the splendours of that large estate. When her father, Baron Nathan, the millionaire Jew banker, suddenly died after being confined by paralysis to his sumptuous mansion in the Champs Élysées, he had long ceased to see her; and he left her as little as possible of his fortune, slices of which had already gone to all sorts of aristocratic charitable enterprises, and even to certain ladies of society who, during the final years of his life, had procured him the illusion of imagining that he had become really one of their set, and was quite cleansed of all his Jewry. However, his supine and indolent daughter, who had never known a passion in her life, not even one for money, paid due honour to his memory, even ordering Masses to be said for his soul, by way of compelling heaven to admit him within its precincts; for, as she often repeated, he had rendered quite enough services to Catholicism to be entitled to a place on the Deity's right hand. And now, having no children, Léa led a lonely life at La Désirade, which remained empty and deathly, enclosed on every side by walls and railings, which shut out the public as if it were some forbidden paradise. Yet there were rumours to the effect that, on the closing of the College of Valmarie, the Countess had granted an asylum to her old friend Father Crabot, who had now reached a very great age. His removal to La Désirade was said by some to be a mere change of cell, for in an ascetic spirit he was content to occupy a little garret formerly assigned to a servant, and furnished with merely an iron bedstead, a deal table, and a rush-seated chair. But he none the less reigned over the estate, as if he were its sovereign master; the only visitors being a few priests and other clerics, who came to take counsel of him, and whose gowns might be seen occasionally gliding between the clumps of verdure or past the marble basins and their plashing waters. Though his ninetieth year was past, Crabot, ever a conqueror of women, a bewitcher of pious souls, repeated the triumphant stroke of his earlier days. He had lost Valmarie, that royal gift, which he had owed to the love of the Countess de Quédeville, but he won La Désirade from the good grace of that ever-beautiful Léa, whom he so fervently called 'my sister Marie in Jesus Christ.' As manager and almoner he set his hands on her fortune, financing all sorts of religious enterprises, and subscribing lavishly to the funds which the reactionary parties established for the purpose of carrying on their desperate campaign against the Republic and its institutions. And thus, when the Countess was found dead on her couch one evening, looking as if in her indolence she had just fallen asleep, she was ruined; her millions had all passed into the cash-boxes of the Black Band, and there only remained the estate of La Désirade, which was willed to Father Crabot on the one condition that he should there establish some such Christian enterprise as he might choose to select.

But these were merely the last convulsions of an expiring world. All Maillebois was now passing into the hands of those Socialists whom the pious dames of other times had pictured as bandits, cut-throats, and footpads. That whilom clerical centre had now gone so completely over to the cause of reason that not a single reactionary member remained in its Municipal Council. Both Philis, once the priests' mayor, and Darras, the so-called traitors' mayor, were dead, and the latter, who was remembered as a man of weak, timorous, hesitating mind, had been replaced by a mayor of great good sense and industrious energy; this being Jules Savin, the younger brother of the twins, those mediocrities, Achille and Philippe. Jules, after marrying a peasant girl named Rosalie Bonin, had worked most courageously, in fifteen years establishing an admirable model farm, which had revolutionised the agricultural methods of the region and greatly increased its wealth. He was now barely more than forty years old, and rather stubborn by nature, for he only yielded to substantial arguments which tended to the general good. And it was under his presidency that the Municipal Council at last found itself called upon to examine a scheme for offering some public reparation to Simon—that idea which had slumbered for a few years, and which now awoke once more.

The subject had frequently been mentioned to Marc, who, indeed, could never come to Maillebois without encountering somebody who spoke to him about it. In this respect he was particularly moved one day when he happened to meet Adrien Doloir, a son of his former pupil Auguste by his wife Angèle. Adrien, after studying successfully under Joulic, had become an architect of great merit, and though barely eight and twenty years of age, had been lately elected to the Municipal Council; of which, indeed, he was the youngest member, one whose schemes were said to be somewhat bold, though none the less practical.

'Ah! my dear Monsieur Froment, how pleased I am to meet you!' he exclaimed as he accosted Marc. 'It so happens that I wished to go over to Jonville to speak to you.'

Like all the young men of the new generation, who loved and venerated Marc as a patriarch, as one of the great workers of the heroic times, Adrien addressed him most deferentially, standing uncovered, with his hat in his hand. Personally, he had only been a pupil of Marc for a very brief period, when he was very young indeed; but his brother and his uncles had all grown up in the old master's class.

'What do you desire of me, my dear lad?' inquired Marc, who felt both brightened and moved whenever he met any of his former boys or their children.

'Well, it is like this. Can you tell me if it is true that the Simon family will soon return to Maillebois? It is said that Simon and his brother David have decided to quit the Pyrenees and settle here again.... Is it true? You must be well acquainted with their views.'

'Such is certainly their intention,' Marc responded with his pleasant smile. 'But I do not think one can expect them till next year; for, though they have found a purchaser for their marble quarry, they are to carry it on for another twelvemonth. Besides, a variety of matters will have to be settled, and they themselves cannot yet tell exactly how and when they will install themselves here.'

'But if we have only a year before us,' exclaimed Adrien with sudden excitement, 'we shall barely have the necessary time for the realisation of a plan I have formed.... I wish to submit it to you before doing anything decisive. What day would be convenient for me to call on you at Jonville?'

Marc, who intended to spend the day at Maillebois with his daughter Louise, pointed out that it would be preferable to profit by this opportunity, and Adrien assenting, it was eventually arranged that he should call at the latter's house in the afternoon. This house was a pleasant dwelling, built by Adrien himself on one of the fields of the farm which had belonged to the old Bongards, in the outskirts of Maillebois. They had long been dead, and the property had remained in the hands of Fernand, the father of Claire, to whom Adrien was married. Thus many memories arose in Marc's mind when, with a still firm and brave step, he walked past the old farm-buildings on his way to the architect's little house. Had he not repaired to that same spot forty years previously—on the very day, indeed, of Simon's arrest—with the object of collecting information in his friend's favour? In imagination Marc again accosted Bongard, the stoutly built and narrow-minded peasant, and his bony and suspicious wife, and found them both stubbornly determined to say nothing, for fear lest they might compromise themselves. He well remembered that he had been unable to extract anything from them, incapable as they were of any act of justice, since they knew nothing and would learn nothing, being, so to say, only so much brute matter steeped in a thick layer of ignorance.

With a sigh, Marc passed on and rang at the gate of Adrien's house. The young architect was awaiting him under an old apple tree, whose strong branches, laden with fruit, sheltered a few garden chairs and a table. 'Ah, master!' Adrien exclaimed, 'what an honour you do me by coming to sit here for a little while! But I have another favour to ask of you. You must kiss my little Georgette, for it will bring her good luck!'

Beside Adrien was Claire, his wife, a smiling blonde, scarcely in her twenty-fourth year, with a limpid face and eyes all intelligence and kindness. It was she who presented the little girl, a pretty child, fair like her mother, and already very knowing for her five years.

'You must remember, my treasure, that Monsieur Froment has kissed you, for it will make you glorious all your life!'

'Oh, I know, mamma! I often hear you talk of him,' said Georgette. 'It is as if a little of the sun came down to see me.'

At this the others began to laugh; but all at once Claire's father and mother, Fernand Bongard and his wife Lucille, made their appearance, having heard that the old schoolmaster intended to call, and wishing to show him some politeness. Although Fernand, with his hard nut, had been anything but a satisfactory pupil in bygone years, Marc was pleased to see him once more. The farmer, now near his fiftieth year, still looked very dull and heavy, as if he were scarcely awake, and his manner remained an uneasy one.

'Well, Fernand,' Marc said to him, 'you ought to be pleased; this has been a good year for the grain crops.'

'Yes, Monsieur Froment, there's some truth in that. But the year's never a really good one. When things go well in one respect they go badly in another. And, besides, I never had any luck, you know.'

His wife, whose mind was sharper than his, thereupon ventured to intervene. 'He says that, Monsieur Froment, because he always used to be the last of his class, and because he imagines that a spell was cast on him by some gipsy when he was quite a little child. A spell, indeed! As if there were any sense in such an idea! It would be different if he believed in the devil, for there is a devil sure enough. Mademoiselle Rouzaire, whose best pupil I was, showed him to me one day, a short time before my first Communion.'

Then, as Claire made merry over this statement, and even little Georgette laughed very irreverently at the idea of there being any such thing as a devil, Lucille continued: 'Oh! I know that you believe in nothing. None of the young folks of nowadays have any religious principles left. Mademoiselle Mazeline made strong-minded women of you all. Nevertheless, one evening, as I well remember, Mademoiselle Rouzaire showed us a shadow passing over the wall, and told us it was the devil. And it was, indeed!'

Adrien, somewhat embarrassed by his mother-in-law's chatter, now interrupted her, and addressed Marc on the subject of his visit. They had all seated themselves, Claire taking Georgette on her lap, while her father and mother kept a little apart from the others, the former smoking his pipe and the latter knitting a stocking.

'Well, master, this is the question,' said Adrien. 'Many young people of the district feel that great dishonour will rest on the name of Maillebois as long as the town has not repaired, as well as it can, the frightful iniquity which it allowed, and in which, indeed, it became an accomplice, when Simon was condemned. His legal acquittal does not suffice; for us—the children and grandchildren of the persecutors—it is a duty to confess and efface the transgression of our forerunners. Yesterday evening, at my father's house, on seeing my grandfather and my uncles there, I again asked them: "How was it that you ever allowed such stupid and monstrous iniquity, when the exercise of a little reason ought to have sufficed to prevent it?" And, as usual, they made vague gestures and answered that they did not know, that they could not know.'

Silence fell, and all eyes turned towards Fernand, who belonged to the incriminated generations. But he likewise rid himself of the question by taking his pipe from his mouth and gesticulating in an embarrassed way, while he remarked: 'Well, to be sure, we didn't know—how could we have known? My father and mother could scarcely sign their names, and they were not so imprudent as to meddle in their neighbours' affairs, for they might have got punished for it. And though I had learnt rather more than they had, I wasn't learned by any means; and so I distrusted the whole business, for a man does not care to risk his skin and his money when he feels he is ignorant.... To you young men nowadays it seems very easy to be brave and wise, because you've been well taught. But I should have liked to have seen you as we were—with no means of telling right from wrong, with our minds at sea amid a lot of affairs in which nobody could distinguish anything certain.'

'That's true,' said Lucille. 'I never thought myself a fool, but all the same I could not understand much of that business, and I tried not to think of it, for my mother was always repeating that poor folk ought not to meddle with the affairs of the rich, unless they wanted to get poorer still.'

Marc had listened with silent gravity. All the past came back: he heard old Bongard and his wife refuse to answer him, like the illiterate peasants they were, whose one desire was to continue toiling and moiling in quietude; and he also remembered Fernand's demeanour on the morrow of the trial at Rozan, when he had still shrugged his shoulders, still persisted in his desire to know nothing. How many years and what prolonged teaching of human reason and civic courage had been needed before a new generation had at last opened its eyes to truth, dared to recognise and admit it! And as Marc looked at Fernand he began to nod, as if to say that he thought the farmer's excuses good ones; for he was already inclined to forgive those persecutors whose ignorance had been the chief cause of their crime. And he ended by smiling at Georgette, in whom, on the other hand, the future seemed to be flowering, as she sat there with her beautiful eyes wide open and her keen ears on the alert, waiting, one might have thought, for some fine story.

'And so, master,' Adrien resumed, 'my plan is a very simple one. As you are aware, some great improvements have been effected at Maillebois lately, with the view of rendering the old quarter of the town more salubrious. An avenue has replaced those sewers, the Rue Plaisir and the Rue Fauche, while on the site of the filthy Rue du Trou is a recreation-ground, which the children of the neighbourhood fill with their play and their laughter. Well, among the building land in front of that square is the very spot on which stood old Lehmann's wretched house, that house of mourning, which our forerunners used to stone. It is my idea, then, to propose to the Municipal Council the erection of a new house on that site—not a palace, but a modest, bright, cheerful dwelling, which might be offered to Simon, so that he might end his days in it encompassed by the respect and affection of everybody. The gift would have no great pecuniary value—it would simply represent delicate and brotherly homage.'

Tears had risen to the eyes of Marc, who was greatly touched by the kind thought thus bestowed on his old friend, the persecuted, innocent man.

'Do you approve of my idea?' inquired Adrien, who on his side was stirred by the sight of Marc's emotion.

The old schoolmaster rose and embraced him: 'Yes, my lad, I approve of it, and I owe you one of the greatest joys of my life.'

'Thank you, master. But that is not everything. Wait a moment. I wish to show you a plan of the house, which I have already prepared, for I should like to direct the work gratuitously, and I feel certain that I should find contractors and men prepared to undertake the building at very low rates.'

He withdrew for a moment, and on returning with the plan he spread it out upon the garden-table, under the old apple tree. And everybody approached and leant over to examine it. The house, such as it had been depicted, was, indeed, a very simple but also a very pleasant one, two storeys high, with a white frontage, and a garden enclosed by some iron railings. Above the entrance a marble slab was figured.

'Is there to be an inscription, then?' Marc inquired.

'Certainly; the house is intended for one. This is what I shall suggest to the Council: "Presented by the Town of Maillebois to Schoolmaster Simon, in the name of Truth and Justice, and in reparation for the torture inflicted on him." And the whole will be signed: "The Grandchildren of his Persecutors."'

With gestures of protest and anxiety Fernand and Lucille glanced at their daughter Claire. Surely that was going too far! She must not let her husband compromise himself to such a point! But Claire, who was leaning lovingly against Adrien's shoulder, smiled, and responded to the consternation of her parents by saying: 'I helped to prepare the inscription, Monsieur Froment; I should like that to be known.'

'Oh! I will make it known, you may depend on it,' Marc answered gaily. 'But the inscription must be accepted, and, first of all, there is the question of the house.'

'Quite so,' replied Adrien. 'I wished to show you my plan with the view of securing your approval and help. The question of the expense will hardly affect the Council. I am more apprehensive of certain scruples, some last attempts at resistance, inspired by the old spirit. Though the members of the Council are nowadays all convinced of Simon's innocence, some of them are timid men, who will only yield to the force of public opinion. And our Mayor, Jules Savin, has said to me, truly enough, that it is essential the scheme should be voted unanimously on the day it is brought forward.'

Then, as a fresh idea occurred to him, Adrien added: 'Do you know, master, as you have been good enough to come so far, you ought to cap your kindness by accompanying me to Jules Savin's at once. He was a pupil of yours, and I feel certain that our cause would make great progress if you would only have a short chat with him.'

'I will do so willingly,' Marc answered. 'Let us start; I will go wherever you like.'

Fernand and Lucille protested no longer. She had returned to her knitting, while he, pulling at his pipe, relapsed into the indifference of a dullard unable to understand the new times. Claire, however, suddenly had to defend the plan from the enterprising hands of little Georgette, who wished to appropriate 'the pretty picture.' Then, as Marc and Adrien made ready to go, there came more embraces, handshakes, and laughter.

The farm of Les Amettes, where Jules Savin resided, was on the other side of Maillebois, and in order to reach it Marc and the young architect had to pass the new recreation-ground. For a moment, therefore, they paused before the plot of land on which the architect proposed to build the projected house.

'You see,' said he, 'all the requirements for a house will be found united here— —'

But he broke off on seeing a stout and smiling man approach him. 'Why, here's uncle Charles!' he exclaimed. 'I say, uncle, when we build the house for Simon the martyr, which I have told you about, you will undertake to provide all the locksmith's work at cost price, will you not?'

'Well, I don't mind, my boy, if it pleases you,' said Charles Doloir. 'And I'll do it also for your sake, Monsieur Froment, for it pains me at times to think of how I used to worry you.'

Charles, after marrying Marthe Dupuis, his employer's daughter, had for a long time been managing the business. He had a son named Marcel, who was about the same age as Adrien, and who, having married a carpenter's daughter, Laure Dumont, had become a contractor for house carpentry.

'I am going to your father's,' Charles resumed, addressing his nephew; 'I have an appointment with Marcel about some work. Come with me, for if you build this house you will have some work to give them as well.... And you will come also, Monsieur Froment? It will please you, perhaps, to meet some more of your old pupils.'

'Yes, indeed it will,' Marc answered gaily. 'Besides, we shall be able to settle the specifications.'

'The specifications! Oh! we have not got to that point yet,' Adrien retorted. 'Moreover, my father isn't an enthusiast.... But no matter; I'll go to see him.'

Auguste Doloir, thanks to the friendly protection of Darras; the former mayor, had become a building contractor in a small way. After his father's death he had taken his mother to live with him, and since the demolition of the Rue Plaisir he had been residing in the new avenue, where he occupied a ground floor flanked by a large yard, in which he stored some of his materials. The lodging was very clean, very healthy, and full of sunlight.

When Marc found himself in the bright dining-room, face to face with Madame Doloir the elder, some more memories of the past returned to him. The old woman, now sixty-nine years old, had retained the demeanour of a good and prudent housewife, one who was instinctively conservative, and allowed neither her husband nor her children to compromise themselves by dabbling in politics. Marc also recalled her husband, Doloir the mason, that big, fair, ignorant fellow, good-natured in his way, but spoilt by barrack-life, haunted as he was by idiotic notions of the army being disorganised by those who knew no country, and of France being sold to the foreigners by the Jews. One day, unfortunately, he had been brought home dead on a stretcher, after falling from a scaffolding; and it seemed as if he had been drinking previously, though Madame Doloir would not acknowledge it, for she was one of those who never admit the existence of family failings.

On perceiving Marc she at once said to him: 'Ah! monsieur, we are no longer young; we are very old acquaintances indeed. Auguste and Charles were not more than eight and six years old when I first saw you.'

'Quite so, madame; I well remember it. I called on you, on behalf of my colleague Simon, to ask you to let your boys tell the truth if they should be questioned.'

At this, though the case was now such a very old one, Madame Doloir became grave and suspicious. 'That affair was no concern of ours,' she answered, 'and I acted rightly in refusing to let it enter our home, for it did great harm to many people.'

Charles, however, perceiving his brother Auguste in the yard with Marcel, ready for the appointment, now called him into the room: 'Come here a moment; I've brought somebody to see you. Besides, your son Adrien is here, and wants to give us an order.'

Auguste, who was as tall and sturdy as his father had been, pressed Marc's hand vigorously. 'Ah, Monsieur Froment,' said he, 'we often talk about you—Charles and I—when we remember our school-days! I was a very bad pupil, and I've regretted it at times. Yet I hope I haven't disgraced you too much; and, in any case, my son Adrien is becoming a man after your own heart.' Then he added, laughing: 'I know what Adrien's order is! Yes, indeed, the house which he wants to build for your friend Simon!... All the same, a house is perhaps a good deal to give to an ex-convict.'

In spite of the bantering *bonhomie* of Auguste's tone, Marc felt grieved by that last remark. 'Do you still think Simon guilty?' he inquired. 'At one time you became convinced of his innocence. But you began to doubt it again after that monstrous trial at Rozan.'

'Well, of course, Monsieur Froment, one feels impressed when a man is found guilty by two juries in succession.... But no! I no longer say that he was the culprit. And besides, at bottom it is all one to us. We are even quite willing that a present should be made to him, if by that means the affair can be brought to an end once and for all, so that we shall never have it dinned into our ears again. Isn't that so, brother?'

'That's correct,' responded Charles. 'If those big fellows were listened to, we ourselves should be the only real criminals, on the ground that we tolerated the injustice. It vexes me. There must be an end to it all!'

The two cousins, Adrien and Marcel, who took an equally passionate interest in the affair, laughed triumphantly. 'So it is settled!' exclaimed Marcel, as he tapped his father on the shoulder. 'You will take charge of the locksmith's work, uncle Auguste of the masonry, and I of the timber work. In that way your share in the crime, as you put it, will be repaired. And we will never mention the matter to you again, we swear it!'

Adrien was laughing and nodding his approval when old Madame Doloir, who had remained standing there, stiff and silent, intervened in her obstinate way. 'Auguste and Charles,' said she, 'have nothing to repair. It will never be known whether Schoolmaster Simon was guilty or not. We little folk ought never to poke our noses into affairs which only concern the Government. And I pity you boys—yes, both of you, Adrien and Marcel—if you imagine that you are strong enough to change things. You fancy that you now know everything, whereas you know nothing at all.... For instance, my poor dead husband, your grandfather, knew that a general meeting of all the Jew millionaires was held in Paris, in a subterranean gallery near the fortifications, every Saturday, when it was decided what sums should be paid to the traitors who betrayed France to Germany. And he knew the story to be a true one, for it had been told him by his own captain, who vouched for it on his honour.'

Marc gazed at the old woman in wonderment, for it was as if he had been carried forty years back. He recognised in her tale one of those extraordinary stories which Doloir the mason had picked up while he was soldiering. For their part, Auguste and Charles had listened to the anecdote in quite a serious way, without any sign of embarrassment, for it was amid similar imbecilities that they had spent their childhood. But neither Adrien nor Marcel could refrain from smiling, however great might be their affectionate deference for their grandmother.

'The Jew syndicate in a cellar! Ah, what an idea, grandmother!' said Adrien softly. 'There are no more Jews, for there will soon be no more

Catholics... The disappearance of the Churches means the end of all religious warfare.'

Then, as his mother now came into the room, he went to kiss her. Angèle Bongard, who had married Auguste Doloir when a shrewd young peasant girl, had largely contributed to her husband's success, though she had no very exceptional gifts. She now at once asked for news of her brother Fernand, her sister-in-law Lucille, and their daughter Claire, Who had married her son. Then the whole family became interested in the latest addition to its number, this being a baby-boy named Célestin, to whom Marcel's wife had given birth a fortnight previously.

'You see, Monsieur Froment,' remarked old Madame Doloir, 'I have become a great-grandmother for the second time; after Georgette has come this little fellow, Célestin. My younger son, Léon, also has a big boy, Edmond, now twelve years old; but he is only my grandson, so with him I don't seem to be quite so old.'

The old woman was becoming amiable—anxious, it seemed, to efface the recollection of her former stiffness, for she continued: 'And, by the way, Monsieur Froment, we never seem to agree; but there is one thing for which I really have to thank you, and that is for having almost compelled me to make Léon a schoolmaster. I didn't care for that profession, for it seemed to me hardly a tempting one; but you took all sorts of pains; you gave lessons to Léon, and now, though he's not yet forty, he already has a good position.'

She had become, indeed, very proud of her youngest son, Léon, who had lately succeeded Sébastien Milhomme in the headmastership of a school at Beaumont, Sébastien having been appointed director of the Training College. The schoolmistress whom Léon had married, Juliette Hochard, had also been transferred to Beaumont, there taking the former post of Mademoiselle Rouzaire; and their eldest son, Edmond, now a pupil at the Lycée, was studying brilliantly.

Well pleased at seeing his grandmother so amiable with Marc, Adrien kissed her, and then said jestingly: 'That's very nice of you, grandmother; you are now on Monsieur Froment's side. And, do you know, on the day when Simon returns we will choose you to offer him a bouquet at the railway station.'

But she again became grave and suspicious. 'Ah, no; not that; certainly not! I don't want to get myself into trouble. You young men are mad with your new ideas!'

After a merry leave-taking, Adrien and Marc at last retired in order to make their way to Jules Savin's. The model farm of Les Amettes spread over some two hundred and fifty acres in the outskirts of Maillebois, just beyond the new district. Jules, after his mother's death, had given a home to his father, the former petty clerk, who was now seventy-one years old; and he had been obliged to do the same for his elder brother, Achille, one of the twins, who, after being for many years a clerk like his father, had been suddenly stricken with paralysis. Philippe, the other twin, and at one time the partner of Jules, was now dead.

It so happened that Marc had become a connection of this family by reason of the marriage of his son Clément with Charlotte, the daughter of Hortense Savin, who had died some years previously. But the marriage had taken place somewhat against Marc's desires, and thus, while allowing Clément all latitude to follow the dictates of his heart, he had preferred personally to hold aloof. He was too broad-minded to make Charlotte responsible for the flighty conduct of her mother, who, after being led astray in her sixteenth year and marrying her seducer, had ended by eloping with another lover, meeting at last with a wretched death in some other part of France. And thus, while imputing nothing to her daughter, Marc harboured certain prejudices against the Savin family generally, and, whatever alacrity he had professed, it had been necessary for him to do violence to his feelings when Adrien had begged him to go to Les Amettes.

As it happened Jules was not at home, but his return was expected every moment. In the meantime the visitors found themselves in the presence of Savin senior, who was watching over his son Achille in a little sitting-room, where the paralysed man now spent his life in an armchair placed near the window. Directly Savin senior caught sight of Marc he raised a cry of surprise: 'Ah! Monsieur Froment,' said he, 'I thought you were angry with me. Well, it is kind of you to call.'

He was still as thin and as puny as ever, still racked, too, by a dreadful cough, yet he had contrived to survive his fresh, pretty, and plump wife, whom, indeed, he had killed by dint of daily vexations inspired by his bitter jealousy.

'Angry?' Marc quietly responded. 'Why should I be angry with you, Monsieur Savin?'

'Oh! because our ideas have never been the same,' said the ex-clerk. 'Your son may have married my granddaughter, but that does not suffice to reconcile our opinions.... For instance, you and your friends are now driving away all the priests and monks, which I regard as very unfortunate, for it will only lead to an increase of immorality. Heaven knows that I don't like those gentry, for I am an old Republican, a Socialist—yes, a Socialist, Monsieur

Froment! But then, women and children need the threats of religion to check them from evil courses, as I have never grown tired of saying.'

An involuntary smile escaped Marc as he listened. Religion a police service!' said he; 'I know your theory. But how can religion exercise any power when people no longer believe, and there is no longer any reason to fear the priests?'

'No longer a reason to fear them!' cried Savin. 'Good Heavens! you are much mistaken. I myself have always been one of their victims. If I had sided with them, do you think that I should have vegetated all my life in a little office, and now be a charge on my son Jules, after losing my wife, who was killed by all sorts of privations? And my son Achille, whom you see here, so grievously afflicted—he again is a victim of the priests. I ought to have sent him to a seminary, and he would now be a prefect or a judge, instead of having contracted all sorts of aches and pains in a horrible office, which he left unable to use either his legs or his arms, so that now he cannot even take a basin of soup unassisted.... The priests are dirty scamps; is it not so, Achille? But all the same, it is better to have them on one's side than against one.'

The cripple, who had greeted his old master with a friendly nod, now remarked slowly, his speech being already impeded by paralysis: 'The priests long controlled the weather, no doubt; nevertheless, one is beginning to do without them very well.' Then, with something like a sneer, he added: 'And so it has become easy enough to settle their account, and play the judge.'

As he spoke he looked at Adrien, for whom that uncomplimentary allusion was doubtless intended. Achille's unfortunate position, the death of his wife, and a quarrel which had arisen between him and his daughter Léontine, who was married to a Beaumont ironmonger, had embittered his nature. And deeming his allusion insufficient, wishing to be more precise, he continued: 'You will remember, Monsieur Froment, that I told you I was still convinced of Simon's innocence at the time when he was recondemned at Rozan. But what could I do? Could I have made a revolution by myself? No, of course not; so it was best to remain silent.... Nevertheless, I now see a number of young gentlemen calling us cowards, and trying to give us a lesson by raising triumphal arches to the martyr. It is brave work indeed!'

On being challenged in this fashion Adrien immediately understood that Jules Savin must have spoken of the great plan. And instead of losing his temper he strove to be very amiable and conciliatory: 'Oh! everybody is brave on becoming just,' he replied. 'I know very well, monsieur, that you were always among the reasonable folk, and I confess that some members of my own family showed even greater blindness and obstinacy than others. But to-day the general desire ought to be to unite, so that all may mingle in the same flame of solidarity and justice.'

Savin senior, who had been listening with an air of stupefaction, now suddenly understood why Marc and Adrien were there, awaiting the return of his son Jules. At the outset he had attributed their visit to politeness only. 'Ah! of course, you have come about that stupid scheme for offering reparation,' said he. 'Well, like those relatives you speak of, I have nothing to do with that business! No, indeed! My son Jules will act as he pleases, of course; but that will not prevent me from keeping my own opinion.... The Jews, monsieur, the Jews, always the Jews!'

Adrien looked at him, in his turn full of stupefaction. The Jews, indeed! Why did he speak of the Jews! Anti-Semitism was dead—to such a degree, indeed, that the new generation failed to understand what was meant when people accused the Jews of every crime. As Adrien had said to his grandmother, Madame Doloir, there were no Jews left, since only citizens, freed from the tyranny of dogmas, remained. It was essentially the Roman Church which had exploited anti-Semitism, in the hope of thereby winning back the incredulous masses; and anti-Semitism had disappeared when that Church sank into the darkness of expiring religions.

Marc had followed the scene with great interest, comparing the past with the present, recalling the incidents and the words of forty years ago, the better to discern the moral of those of to-day. However, Jules Savin at last came in, accompanied by his son Robert, a tall youth of sixteen, whom he was already initiating into the farmwork. And directly he learnt the purpose of his visitors he appeared to be much touched, and addressing Marc with great deference, exclaimed:

'Monsieur Froment, you cannot doubt my desire to be agreeable to you. We all regard you nowadays as a just and venerable master. Besides, as my friend Adrien must have told you, I am in no sense opposed to his plan. On the contrary, I will employ all the authority I possess to second it, for I am entirely of his opinion. Maillebois will only regain its honour when it has offered reparation for its fault.... Only, I repeat it, there must be absolute unanimity in the Municipal Council. I am working in that sense, and I beg you to do the same.'

Then, as his father began to sneer, Jules said to him, smiling: 'Come, don't pretend to be so hard-headed; you admitted Simon's innocence to me the other day.'

'His innocence? Oh! I don't dispute that. I also am innocent, but nobody builds me a house.'

'You have mine,' Jules retorted somewhat roughly.

At bottom it was precisely that circumstance which hurt Savin's feelings. The hospitality he received at his son's house, the fate that had befallen him of ending his days peacefully, in the home of one who had succeeded by dint of great personal efforts, gave the lie to his everlasting recriminations, the regret he was always expressing at not having sided with the priests in spite of the hatred with which he regarded them. Thus, losing his temper, he cried: 'Well, if you choose you can build a cathedral for your Simon! It won't matter to me, for I shall stay at home.'

Then Achille, who, tortured by the pains in his legs, had just raised a pitiful moan, exclaimed: 'Alas! I shall stay at home as well. But if I were not nailed to this armchair I would willingly go with you, my dear Jules, for I belong to the generation which did not, perhaps, do all its duty, but which was not ignorant of it, and is ready to do it now.'

After those words Marc and Adrien withdrew, delighted, feeling certain of success. And when Marc found himself alone again, returning to his daughter Louise by way of the broad thoroughfares of the new district, he summed up all he had just seen and heard; the far-off memories, which at the same time returned to him, enabling him to gauge the distance which had been travelled during the last forty years. The whole story of his life, his efforts and his triumph, was spread out, and he felt that he had been right in former days, when he had said that if France did not protest and rise to do justice in the Simon case, it was because she was steeped in too much ignorance, because she was debased and poisoned by religious imbecility and malice, because she was kept in childish superstitions and notions by a Press given over to lucre, scandal, and blackmailing. And, in the same way, a clear intuition had come to him of the only possible remedy—instruction, education, which would liberate one and all, endow them with solidarity and the intelligent bravery of life, by killing falsehood, destroying error, sweeping away the senseless dogmas of the Church, with its hell, its heaven, and its doctrines of social death. That was what Marc had desired, and that, indeed, was the work which was being accomplished—the liberation of the people by the primary schools, the rescue of all citizens from the state of iniquity in which they had been plunged, in order that they might at last become capable of truth and justice.

But it was particularly a feeling of appeasement which now came over Marc. Only forgiveness, tolerance, and kindliness surged from his heart. In former times he had greatly suffered, and he had often felt passionately angry with men on seeing with what stupid cruelty they behaved, and how obstinately they persisted in evil. At present, however, he could not forget the words spoken by Fernand Bongard and Achille Savin. They had tolerated injustice, no doubt; but as they now said, this was because they had not known, and because they had not felt strong enough to contend with that injustice. The slumber of their intelligence could not be imputed to the disinherited scions of ignorance as a crime. And Marc willingly forgave one and all; he no longer harboured any rancour even against the obstinate ones, who refused to open their minds to facts; he would simply have liked the festival planned for Simon's return to become a festival of general reconciliation, one in which the whole of Maillebois would embrace and mingle in brotherly concord, resolving to work henceforth for the happiness of all.

On reaching Louise's quarters at the school, where Geneviève had awaited him, and where they were to dine in company with Clément, Charlotte, and Lucienne, Marc was pleased to find that Sébastien and Sarah were also there, having just arrived from Beaumont to share the meal. Indeed, it was a general family gathering, and several leaves had to be added to the table. There were Marc and Geneviève; then Clément and Charlotte, with their daughter Lucienne, who was already seven years old; then Joseph Simon and Louise; then Sébastien Milhomme and Sarah; then François Simon, Joseph's son, and Thérèse Milhomme, Sarah's daughter, two cousins who had married, and who were already the parents of a little two-year-old named Rose. Altogether they made a dozen, full of health and appetite.

Acclamations arose when Marc recounted his afternoon, describing Adrien's plan and expressing his belief in its success. Joseph alone felt doubtful, for he was not convinced, he said, of the Mayor's favourable disposition. But Charlotte immediately intervened. 'You are mistaken,' she exclaimed; 'my uncle Jules is altogether on our side.... We can rely on him. He is the only one of the family who ever showed me any kindness.'

Charlotte, it should be said, had become dependent on her grandfather, Savin senior, at the time when her mother had eloped, for it had become necessary to place her father in an asylum on account of the alcoholism to which he had given way. The girl had then experienced much suffering, being often cuffed and sparsely fed. Savin, who seemed oblivious of the deplorable result of the pious hypocrisy in which his daughter Hortense had been reared by Mademoiselle Rouzaire, accused his grandchild of being an atheist, a rebel, full of deplorable ways, which were due to the teaching of Mademoiselle Mazeline. As a matter of fact, however, Charlotte was delightful, free from all false prudery, and gifted with healthy uprightness, sense, and tenderness. And Clément having married her in spite of all obstacles, they had since lived together in the happiest and the closest of unions.

'Charlotte is right,' said Marc, who also desired to defend Jules Savin; 'the Mayor is on our side. But the best of all is that, among the contractors for the house which it is proposed to present to Simon, there will be the two Doloirs, Auguste the mason and Charles the locksmith; besides which, by their ties of relationship, even Fernand Bongard and Achille Savin will be indirectly concerned in it.... Ah! Sébastien, my friend, who would have thought that would come to pass in the days when you and those fine fellows attended my school?'

At this sally Sébastien Milhomme began to laugh; though his mood was scarcely a cheerful one, for a recent family loss, a very tragical affair, had affected him painfully. During the previous spring his aunt, Madame Edouard, had died, leaving the stationery business to her sister-in-law, Madame Alexandre. Her son Victor having disappeared, she had of recent years seemed to waste away, no longer attending to the business, in which she had once taken such a passionate interest, and feeling, indeed, quite at sea amidst those new times, which she altogether failed to understand. Madame Alexandre on remaining alone had continued carrying on the business, for she did not wish to inconvenience her son Sébastien, though the latter's position was becoming extremely good. One evening, however, Victor suddenly reappeared, emerging hungry and sordid from the depths in which he had been leading a crapulous life. He had heard of his mother's death, and he instantly demanded that the business should be put up for sale and the old partnership liquidated, in order that he might carry off his share of the proceeds. Such, then, was the end of the little shop in the Rue Courte, where many generations of schoolboys had purchased their copybooks and their pens. For a short time Victor showed himself here and there in Maillebois, leading a merry life, almost invariably in the company of his old chum, Polydor Souquet, who had fallen to the gutter. One evening Marc, having to cross a street of ill-repute, caught sight of them with another man, whose black figure strikingly resembled that of Brother Gorgias. And finally, barely a week before the family dinner given by Louise, the police had found a man lying dead, with his skull split, outside a haunt of debauchery. The dead man was Victor. There had evidently been some dim, ignoble tragedy, which the interested parties endeavoured to hush up.

'Yes, yes,' said Sébastien in reply to Marc, 'I remember my schoolfellows. With a few unfortunate exceptions they have not turned out so badly. But in life one is at times exposed to certain poisons, which prove pitiless.'

The others did not insist. They preferred to inquire after his mother, whom he had now taken to live with him at the Beaumont Training College, and who still enjoyed good health in spite of her great age. Sébastien's new position gave him a great deal of occupation, particularly as he desired to perfect the work of his venerated master, Salvan. 'Ah!' he exclaimed, 'that public reparation offered to Simon, that glorification of a schoolmaster, will be a great joy for all of us. I want my pupils to participate in it, and for that purpose I shall endeavour to obtain a day's holiday for them.'

Marc, who had rejoiced at Sébastien's appointment as if it were a personal triumph, at once signified his approval. 'Quite so,' said he, 'and we will bring the old ones as well—Salvan, Mademoiselle Mazeline, and Mignot. Besides, speaking of school-teachers, there is already a fine battalion here present.'

The others began to laugh. With the exception of the two children they were, indeed, all teachers. Clément and Charlotte still carried on the Jonville schools, Joseph and Louise had decided that they would never quit Maillebois, Sébastien and Sarah relied on remaining at the Beaumont Training College until the former reached the age limit; while as for the younger couple, François and Thérèse, they had not long been appointed to the Dherbecourt schools, where their parents had previously made their *débuts*. François, in whom one traced a likeness to his parents, Joseph and Louise, also resembled his grandfather Marc, for he had much the same lofty brow and bright eyes, though the latter in his case glowed with what seemed to be a flame of insatiable desire. In Thérèse, on the other hand, one found the great beauty of her mother Sarah softened, quieted, as it were, by the intellectual refinement which she had inherited from her father, Sébastien. And Rose, the young couple's little girl, the last born of the family, and as such worshipped by one and all, seemed to personify the budding future.

The dinner proved delightfully gay. How joyful for Joseph and Sarah, the children of the innocent martyr, tortured for so many years, was the thought of the festival of reparation which was now being planned! Their own children and their grandchild—all that had come from their blood mingled with that of Marc, the martyr's most heroic defender—would participate in that glorification. Four generations, indeed, would be present to celebrate the truth, and the *cortège* would be formed of all the good workers who, having suffered for its sake, were entitled to share its triumph.

Laughter, and again laughter, arose. They all drank to the return of Simon, and even when ten o'clock struck the happy family continued to give expression to its delight, quite forgetful of the trains by which some of its members were to return to Beaumont and others to Jonville.

From that day forward things moved with unexpected rapidity. Adrien's scheme on being laid before the Municipal Council was voted unanimously, as Jules Savin, the Mayor, had desired. Nobody even thought of opposing the suggested inscription. None of the applications and pleadings, which the promoters of the scheme had imagined necessary, were required, for the idea to which they gave expression already existed, in embryo, in the minds of all. There was remorse for the past, uneasiness at the thought of the unhealed iniquity, and a craving to repair it for the sake of the town's honour. Everybody now felt that it was impossible to be happy outside the pale of civic solidarity, for durable happiness can only come to a people when it is just. And so in a few weeks' time the subscription lists were filled. As the amount required was a comparatively small one, being no more than thirty thousand francs, [2] —for the site of the house was given by the municipality,—people contented themselves with subscribing two, three, or at the utmost five francs, in order that a larger number of subscribers might participate. The workmen of the *faubourg* and the peasants of the environs contributed their half-francs and their francs; and at the end of March the building was put in hand, for it was desired that everything should be in readiness, the last woodwork in position, and the last paint dry, by mid-September, the date which Simon had ended by fixing for his return.

[2] $6000.

In September, then, the simple but cheerful house stood completed in its pleasant garden, which was faced by a railing on the side of the square. Its affectionately-awaited owner might come to take possession of it when he pleased, for nothing was lacking. True, a drapery hung before the marble slab bearing an inscription over the doorway; but this inscription, so far as Simon was concerned, was to be the great surprise, and would only be uncovered at the last moment. Adrien repaired to the Pyrenees to plan the final arrangements with Simon and David, and it was then decided that the former's wife, who was in a very weak state of health, should in the first instance install herself in the house, with the help of her children, Joseph and Sarah. Then, on the appointed day, Simon would arrive with his brother David. There would be an official reception at the railway station, and afterwards he would be conducted in triumph to his new home, the gift of his fellow-townsmen, where his wife and children would await him.

At last, on the Twentieth of September, a Sunday, the solemnity was enacted amid radiant sunshine and a warm and pure atmosphere. The streets of Maillebois were decorated with flags, the last flowers of the season were scattered along the procession's line of route. And early in the morning—although the train would only arrive at three o'clock in the afternoon—the population assembled out of doors, gathering together in a happy, singing, laughing multitude, whose numbers were swollen by all the visitors who flocked in from neighbouring parishes. At noon one could no longer circulate outside the house on the large new square, whose recreation-ground was invaded by the working-class families of the neighbourhood. There were people, too, at all the windows, and the very roadways were blocked by waves of spectators eager to see and to cry their passion for justice. Nothing could have been grander or more inspiring.

Marc and Geneviève had arrived from Jonville, with Clément, Charlotte, and little Lucienne, early in the day. It was arranged that they should await Simon in the garden of the house, grouped around Madame Simon, her children, Joseph and Sarah, her grandchildren, François and Thérèse, and her great-granddaughter, little Rose. Louise, of course, was there, beside her husband Joseph, and Sébastien beside his wife Sarah. These constituted the three generations which had sprung from the blood of the innocent man mingled with that of his champions. Then, also, places had been reserved for the first defenders, the survivors of the heroic days,—Salvan, Mademoiselle Mazeline, and Mignot,—as well as for the fervent artisans of the work of reparation, the now conquered and enthusiastic members of the Bongard, Doloir, and Savin families. It was rumoured that Delbos, the ex-advocate, the hero of the two trials, who for four years recently had held the office of Minister of the Interior, had gone to join Simon and David, in order to reach the town in their company. Only the Mayor and a deputation of the Municipal Council were to meet the brothers at the railway station and conduct them to the house, decked with banners and garlands, where the ceremony of presentation would take place. And there, in accordance with this programme, Marc remained waiting with the rest of the family, in spite of all his joyous eagerness to embrace the triumpher.

Two o'clock struck; there was still an hour to be spent patiently. Meanwhile the crowd steadily increased. Marc, having left the garden to mingle with the groups and hear what was being said, found that the one subject of conversation was that extraordinary story emerging from the past, that condemnation of an innocent man, which had become both abominable and inexplicable in the eyes of the new generations. From the younger folk a long cry of indignant amazement arose; while the old people, those who had witnessed the iniquity, tried to defend themselves with vague gestures and shamefaced explanations. Now that the truth had become manifest in the full sunlight, endowed with all the force of invincible certainty, the children and the grandchildren could not understand how their parents and grandparents had carried blindness and egotism so far as to fail to fathom so simple an affair. And doubtless many of the older folk shared the astonishment of the younger ones, and were at a loss to account for the credulity into which they had fallen. That, indeed, was their best answer to the reproaches they heard; it was necessary to have lived in those times to understand the power of falsehood over ignorance. One old man penitently confessed his error; another related how he had hissed Simon on the day of his arrest, and how he had now been waiting two hours in order to acclaim him, anxious as he was not to die with his bad action upon his conscience. And a youth, his grandson, thereupon threw himself on the old man's neck and kissed him, laughing, with tears in his eyes. Marc was delightfully touched by the scene, and continued to walk about, looking and listening.

But all at once he stopped short. He had just recognised Polydor Souquet, clad in rags, with a ravaged countenance, as if still under the effects of a night of intoxication. And Marc was thunderstruck when by the side of Polydor he perceived Brother Gorgias, clad as usual in black, without a sign of linen, his greasy old frock-coat clinging fast to his dark hide. He, Gorgias, was not drunk. Silent and fierce of aspect, erect in all his tragic leanness, he darted fiery glances at the crowd. And Marc could hear that Polydor, with a drunkard's stupid obstinacy, was deriding him respecting the affair, of which everybody was talking around them. Slabbering and stammering, the scamp went on:

'I say, old man, the copy-slip—you remember, eh? The copy-slip! It was I who sneaked it. I had it in my pocket, and I was stupid enough to give it you back while you were seeing me home.... Ah, yes! that wretched copy-slip.'

A sudden flash of light illumined Marc's mind. He now knew the whole truth. The one gap in the affair, which had still worried him occasionally, was now filled. Polydor had given the slip to Gorgias, and that explained how it had chanced to be in his pocket, and how it had become mingled with a copy of *Le Petit Beaumontais* when, terrified by his victim's cries, he had hastily sought a handkerchief, a stopper of any kind, to use as a gag.

'But you know, old man,' stammered Polydor, 'we liked each other very much, and we didn't tell our business to other folk. And yet, if I *had* chattered, what a rumpus there would have been! Ah! what a face my Aunt Pélagie would have pulled!'

Half-fuddled, in an ignoble state, the rascal went on jeering, unconscious, it seemed, of the presence of the people around him. And Gorgias, who from time to time gave him a contemptuous glance, must suddenly have understood that Marc had heard the drunkard's involuntary confession, for in a low voice he growled: 'Be quiet, you wine-bag! Be quiet, you rotten cur! You stink of your sin and mine; you have damned me again by your ignominy! Be quiet, you filthy thing; it is I who will speak! Yes, I will confess my fault, in order that God may pardon me!'

Then, addressing himself to Marc, who was still lost in silent amazement, he went on: 'You heard him, Monsieur Froment, didn't you? Well, it's necessary that all should hear. I have been consumed long enough by a desire to confess myself to men, even as I have confessed to God, in order that my salvation may be the more glorious. And, besides, all these people exasperate me! They know absolutely nothing; they keep on repeating my name with execration, as if I were the only culprit! But wait a moment; they will see it is not so, for I will tell them everything!'

Then, though he was over seventy years old, he contrived to spring upon the low wall supporting the garden railing of the house where Simon, the innocent man, was soon to be received in triumph. And clinging with one hand to that railing, he turned and faced his mighty audience. During the hour he had spent roaming through the groups, he had heard his name fall from every tongue as a name of infamy. And he had gradually been fired by a sombre fever, the bravery of a fine bandit, who denies none of his actions, but is ready to cast them in the teeth of men, full of a mad pride that he should have dared to commit them. What caused him most suffering, however, was that he alone should be named, that all the weight of the general execration should be cast upon his shoulders, for the others, his accomplices, seemed to be quite forgotten. Only the previous day, his resources again being exhausted, he had attempted to force himself upon Father Crabot, who was shut up at the estate of La Désirade, and he had been flung out with the alms of a twenty-franc piece, the very last that would be given him, so he had been told. And now, amid all the insulting words that were levelled at him, nobody shouted the name of Father Crabot. Why, as he was ready to expiate his transgression, why should not Father Crabot expiate his also? No doubt he, Gorgias, would extract no more twenty-franc pieces from that coward if he were to reveal everything; but his hatred was now dearer to him than money, and it would be blissful to cast his enemy into the flames of hell, while he himself ascended to the delights of paradise by virtue of the penance of a public confession, the idea of which had long haunted him.

Thus an unexpected, an extraordinary scene began. With a violent, sweeping gesture, Gorgias sought to gather the crowd together and attract its attention. And in a shrill but still powerful voice he called: 'Listen to me! listen to me! I will tell you everything!'

But at first he was not heard, and he had to raise the same cry twice, thrice, a dozen times, with increasing, unwearying energy. By degrees he was noticed and people became attentive; and when some of the old folk had recognised him, when his name had flown from mouth to mouth amid a quiver of horror, a death-like silence at last fell from one to the other end of the great square.

'Listen to me! listen to me! I will tell you everything!'

Raised above the heads of all the others, with the broad sunlight streaming on him, he clung with one hand to the iron railing, while with the other he went on making vehement gesticulations as if he were sabring the air. His threadbare frock-coat hung closely to his withered, knotty frame, and with his dusky face, from which jutted the big beak of a bird of prey, he looked quite terrible, like some phantom of the past, whose eyes glowed with the flames of all the abominable passions of long ago.

'You speak of truth and justice,' he cried. 'But you know nothing, and you are not just!... You all fall upon me, you treat me as if I were the only culprit, whereas others sinned more even than I did. I may have been a criminal, but others accepted my crime, hid it, and continued it.... Wait a little while; you will see by-and-by that I don't lack the courage to confess my sin. But why am I the only one ready to confess? Why isn't my master, my chief, the all-powerful Father Crabot, here also, ready to humiliate himself and tell everything? Let him come! Go and fetch him from his hiding-place, and let him confess his sins before you and do penitence beside me. Otherwise I shall speak out; I shall proclaim his crime with mine, for though I be the most humble, the most miserable of sinners, God is in me, and it is God who demands expiation of him as of me.'

Then, in the bitterest language, he declared that all his superiors, Father Crabot at the head of them, were but degenerate Catholics, poltroons, and enjoyers of life. The Church was dying by reason of their cowardice, their compromises with the weaknesses and the vanities of the world. It was, indeed, his favourite theory that all true religious spirit had departed from those monks, those priests, and those bishops, who ought to have ensured the reign of Jesus by fire and sword. Earth and mankind belonged to God alone, and God had given them to His Church, the sovereign delegate of His power. The Church therefore possessed everything, and held absolute dominion over everybody and everything. To her belonged the disposal of wealth; none could be wealthy save by her permission. To her belonged even the disposal of life, for every living man was her subject, whom she allowed to live or suppressed according to the interests of Heaven. Such was the doctrine from which the true saints had never departed. He, a mere humble Ignorantine, had always practised and exalted that doctrine, and his superiors, though they had wronged him in other respects, had always recognised in him the rare merit of possessing the true, absolute religious spirit; whereas they themselves—the Crabots, the Philibins, and the Fulgences—had ruined religion by their compromises, their trickery with the Freethinkers, the Jews, the Protestants, and the Freemasons. Like opportunists, anxious to please, they had gradually abandoned dogmas and concealed the asperity of doctrines, whereas they ought to have fought openly against impiety, and have slaughtered and burnt all heretics. He himself dreamt of seeing a huge sacrificial pyre set up in the midst of Paris, on which he would have cast the whole guilty nation, in order that the flames and the stench from all those millions of bodies might have ascended to the glowing skies to rejoice and appease the Deity.

And he next exclaimed: 'As soon as a sinner confesses and does penance, he is no longer guilty, he again recovers the grace of his Sovereign Master. What man is there who never sins? All who are made of flesh are liable to err. Even like the layman, he who is in holy orders and whom the beast, which is in all men, precipitates into crime has but one obligation cast upon him—that of confession; and if he receives absolution, if he expiates his sin with firm repentance, he redeems himself, he becomes again as white as snow, worthy to enter into Heaven, among the roses and lilies of Mary.... I confessed my sin to Father Théodose, who absolved me, and I owed nothing more to anybody, since God, who ordains and knows all things, had pardoned me by the sacrament of one of His ministers. And in the same way, from that day forward, each time that I lied, each time that my superiors compelled me to lie, I went back to the confessional, and I washed my soul clean of all the impurities with which human fragility had soiled it. Alas! I have often and I have greatly sinned, for God, in order no doubt to try me, has allowed the devil to assail me with all the fires of hell. But I have battered my chest with my fists, I have made my knees bleed by dragging them over the flagstones of chapels—I have paid, and I repeat that I owe nothing whatever. A flight of archangels would bear me straight to Paradise if I should die by-and-by, ere lapsing again into the original mire, whence in common with all men I have sprung. And in particular I owe nothing to men; I have never owed them anything; my crime lies between God and me, His servant. But He has forgiven me, and so, if I speak here to-day, it is because I choose to do so, because I desire to couple with the Divine mercy the martyrdom of a last humiliation, in order that I may enter Paradise in triumph—a celestial joy which, whatever my abjection, I shall assuredly taste, thanks to my penitence; whereas you will never taste it—race of unbelievers and blasphemers that you are, destined, one and all, to the flames of hell!'

Amid his sombre fury, that transport of savage faith which had raised him there, alone and impudent, face to face with the multitude, Gorgias again began to jeer. And there came to him that habitual twitching of the lips, which disclosed some of his teeth in a grimace suggestive of both scorn and cruelty. Polydor, who for a moment had seemed quite scared, and had gazed at him with dilated eyes, blurred by his drunkenness, had now fallen beside the railing, overcome by sleepiness and already snoring. The crowd, in horrified expectancy of the promised confession, had hitherto preserved death-like silence. But it was now growing weary of that long oration, in which it found all the unconquerable pride and insolence of the Churchman who deems himself all-powerful and inviolate. What did the scamp mean by that speech? Why did he not content himself with stating the facts? What was the use of such a long preamble when a dozen words would have sufficed? Thus a growl arose, and a rush would have swept Gorgias away if Marc, now very attentive and fully master of himself, had not stepped forward and with a gesture calmed the growing impatience and anger. Moreover, Gorgias remained imperturbable. Despite all interruptions, he went on repeating in the same shrill voice that he alone was brave, that he alone was really upon God's side, and that the other sinners, the cowards, would after all have to pay for their transgressions, since God had set him there to make public confession on their behalf as well as his own, this being a supreme expiation, whence the Church, compromised by her unworthy leaders, would emerge rejuvenated and for ever victorious.

Then all at once, as if he were a prey to the wildest remorse, he beat his chest violently with both fists, and cried in distressful, tearful accents: 'I have sinned, O God! O God, do Thou forgive me! Release me from the claws of the devil, O God, that I may yet bless Thy holy name!... Yes, God wills it! Listen to me, listen to me; I will tell you everything!'

Then he laid himself bare, as it were, before the assembled throng. He spoke plainly of his gross appetites; he set forth that he had been a big eater, a deep drinker, and that vice had dogged him from his childhood. In spite of all his intelligence he had then refused to study; he had preferred to play the truant, to roam the fields, and hide in the woods with little hussies. His father, Jean Plumet, after being a poacher, had been turned into a gamekeeper by the Countess de Quédeville. His mother, a hussy, had disappeared after giving him birth. He could still picture his father as he had appeared to him lying on a stretcher in the courtyard at Valmarie, whither he had been brought dead, after two bullets had been lodged in his chest by one of his former companions, a poacher. And subsequently he, Gorgias, had been brought up with the Countess's grandson, Gaston, an unmanageable lad, who also refused to study, preferring to hide himself away with little hussies, climb poplar trees for magpies' nests, and wade the rivers in search of crawfish. At that time he, Gorgias, had become acquainted with Father Philibin, Gaston's tutor, and Father Crabot, who was then in all his manly prime, adored by the old Countess, and already the real master of Valmarie. Then, with sudden abruptness, plainly and brutally, Gorgias related how Gaston, the grandson and heir, had come by his death—a death which he had witnessed from a distance, and of which he had kept the terrible secret for so many years. The boy had been deliberately pushed into the river and drowned there, the misfortune being attributed to an accident, in such wise that a few months later the old Countess finally bestowed her property upon Father Crabot.

Striking his breast with increasing fury, beside himself with contrition, Gorgias continued amid his sobs: 'I have sinned, I have sinned, O God! And my superiors have sinned still more frightfully than I, for it was they, O God! who ever set me an evil example!... But since I am here to expiate their sins as well as mine by confessing everything, O God, perchance Thou wilt pardon them in Thine infinite mercy, even as Thou wilt assuredly pardon me also!'

But a quiver of indignant revolt now sped through the crowd. Fists were raised and voices demanded vengeance; while Gorgias, resuming his narrative, related that from that time forward Fathers Crabot and Philibin had never abandoned him, linked to him as they were by a bond of blood, relying on him as he relied on them. This was the old pact which Marc had long suspected—Gorgias being admitted to the Church and becoming an Ignorantine, an *enfant terrible* of the Deity, one who both alarmed and enraptured his superiors by the wonderful religious spirit which glowed in his guilty flesh. Again the wretched man sobbed aloud, and all at once he passed to the horrid crime of which Simon had been accused.

'The little angel was there, O God!... It is the truth. I had just taken the other boy home, and I was passing across the dark square, when I saw the little angel in his room, which was lighted up.... Thou God knowest that I approached him without evil intention, simply out of curiosity, and in a fatherly spirit, in order to scold him for leaving his window open. And Thou knowest also that for a while I talked to him as a friend, asking him to show me the pictures on his table, sweet and pious pictures, which were still perfumed by the incense of the first Communion. But why, O God, why didst Thou then allow the devil to tempt me? Why didst Thou abandon me to the tempter, who impelled me to spring over the window-bar under the pretence of taking a closer look at the pictures, though, alas! the flames of hell were already burning within me? Ah! why didst Thou suffer it, O God? Ah! verily, my God, Thy ways are mysterious and terrible!'

The throng had now again relapsed into deathly silence amid the frightful anguish which wrung every breast as the ignoble confession at last took its course. Not a breath was heard; horror spread over all those motionless folk, terrified by the thought of what was coming. And Marc, who was very white, quite scared at seeing the truth rise before him at last, after so many lies, gazed fixedly at the wretched culprit, who was gesticulating frantically amid the sobs which choked him.

'The little child—he was so pretty. Thou hadst given him, O God! the fair and curly head of a little angel. Like the cherubs of pious paintings, he seemed, indeed, to have but that angelic head with two wings.... Kill him, O God! Did I have any such horrible thought? Speak! Thou canst read my heart! I was so fond of him, I would not have plucked a hair from his head.... But it is true the fire of hell had come upon me; Satan transported me, blinded me, and the boy became alarmed; he began to call out, to call out, to call out.... O God, those calls, those calls! I hear them always, always, and they madden me!'

It seemed, indeed, as if Gorgias were now a prey to some supreme paroxysm; his eyes glowed like coals of fire in his convulsed countenance, a little foam appeared upon his twisted lips, while his lean, bent frame quivered from head to foot with spasmodic shocks. And at last a great access of rage transported him. Like one of the damned whom the devil turns with his fork over the infernal brazier, he howled: 'No, no, that's not the plain truth; that again is arranged and embellished.... I must tell all, I will tell all; it is at that price only that I shall taste the eternal delights of Paradise!'

What followed was full of horror. He related everything in plain, crude, abominable language, and when he again came to his victim's cries he recounted his cowardly terror, his eager desire to conceal his crime, for his buzzing ears already seemed to re-echo the gallop of the gendarmes pursuing him. In wild despair he had sought for something; he had searched his pocket, and finding some papers in it, he had stuffed them without foresight or method into his victim's mouth, all eagerness as he was to hear those terrible cries no more. But they had begun again, and he told how he had then murdered, strangled, the boy, pressing his strong, bony, hairy fingers, like iron bands, around the child's delicate neck, and marking it with deep, dark furrows.

'O God!' he cried, 'I am a hog, I am a murderous brute, my limbs are stained with mire and blood!... And I fled like a wretched coward, without an idea in my head, quite brutified and senseless, leaving the window open, and thereby showing my stupidity and the innocence in which I should have remained but for the devil's unforeseen and victorious assault upon me.... And now that I have confessed everything to men, O God, I beg Thee, in reward for my penitence, open to me the doors of Heaven!'

But the horror-fraught patience of the crowd was now exhausted. After the stupor which had kept it chilled and mute there came an outburst of extraordinary violence. A loud roar of imprecations rolled from one to the other end of the square, a huge wave gathered and bounded towards the railings, towards the impudent wretch, the monstrous penitent, who in his religious dementia had thus dared to proclaim his crime in the full sunlight. Shouts arose: 'To death with the scoundrel! To death with the murderer! To death with the polluter and killer of children!' And Marc then understood the terrible danger; he pictured the crowd lynching that wretched man in its craving for immediate justice; he beheld that festival of kindness and solidarity, that triumph of truth and equity, soiled, blackened by the summary execution of the culprit, whose limbs would be torn from him and cast to the four winds of heaven. So in all haste he strove to remove Gorgias from the railings. But he had to contend with his resistance, for the obstinate, frantic scoundrel desired to say something more. At last, helped by the vigorous arms of some of the bystanders, Marc managed to carry him into the garden, the gate of which was at once shut. The rescue was effected none too soon, for the huge wave of the indignant crowd rolled up and burst against the railings, which fortunately checked its further progress, as they were new and strong. Thus Gorgias was for the moment out of reach, sheltered by the very house which had been built for the innocent man, for whose tortures he, was responsible. And such was his obstinacy, that when those who had seized him released their hold, thinking him conquered, he picked himself up, and, rushing back to the railings, hung to them from inside. And there, protected by the iron bars, against which the furious, surging throng was sweeping, he began once more:

'Thou didst witness, O God! my first expiation, when my superiors, as foolish as they were cruel, abandoned me on the road to exile! Thou knowest to what unacknowledgeable callings they reduced me, what fresh and hateful transgressions they caused me to commit! Thou knowest their base avarice—how they refused me even a crust of bread, how they refuse it still, after being my counsellors and accomplices all my life long.... For thou wert always present, O God! Thou didst hear them bind themselves to me. Thou knowest that after my crime I did but obey them, and that if I aggravated it by other crimes it was only by and for them. Doubtless the desire was to save Thy Holy Church from scandal—and I, indeed, would have given my blood, my life. But they thought only of saving their own skins, and it is that which has enraged me and stirred me to tell everything.... And now, O God! that I have been Thy justiciary, that I have spoken the words of violence ordained by Thee, and have cried aloud their unknown and unpunished sins, it is for Thee to decide if Thou wilt pardon them or strike them down in Thy wrath, even before these swinish people, who pretend to forget Thy name, and for the roasting of whose sacrilegious limbs there will never be room enough in hell!'

Threatening hoots interrupted him at every word; stones, passing from hand to hand, began to fly around his head. The railings would not have resisted much longer; in fact, a last great onrush was about to throw them down when Marc and his assistants again managed to seize Gorgias and carry him to the end of the garden, behind the house. On that side there was a little gate conducting to a deserted lane, and the miscreant was soon led forth, and then driven away.

If, however, the growling, threatening crowd suddenly became calm, it was because cries of joy and glorification arose above the shouts of anger, drawing nearer every moment in sonorous waves along the sunlit avenue. Simon, having been received at the railway station by a deputation of the Municipal Council, was arriving in a large landau, he and David occupying the back seat, while in front of them were Advocate Delbos and Jules Savin, the Mayor. As the carriage slowly advanced between the serried crowd there came an extraordinary ovation. Spurred to it by the abominable scene which had left everybody quivering, they acclaimed Simon with the wildest enthusiasm, for his innocence and his heroism seemed to have been rendered yet more glorious by the public confession now made by the real culprit, the savage and bestial Gorgias. Women wept and raised their children to let them see the hero. Men rushed to unharness the horses; and indeed they did unharness them, in such wise that the landau was dragged to the house by a hundred brave arms. And all along the flower-strewn line of route other flowers were flung from the windows, where handkerchiefs as well as banners waved. A very beautiful girl mounted the carriage step, and remained there like a living statue of youth, contributing the splendour of her beauty to the martyr's triumph. Kisses were wafted, words of affection and glorification fell into the carriage with the bouquets which rained from every side. Never had people been stirred by such intense emotion—emotion wrung from their very vitals by the thought of such a great iniquity—emotion which, seeking to bestow some supreme compensation on the victim, found it in the gift without reserve of the hearts and love of all. Glory to the innocent man who had well-nigh perished by the people's fault, and on whom the people would never be able to bestow sufficient happiness! Glory to the martyr who had suffered so greatly for unrecognised and strangled truth, and whose victory was that of human reason freeing itself from the bonds of error and falsehood! And glory to the schoolmaster struck down in his functions, a victim of his efforts to promote enlightenment, and now exalted the more as he had suffered untold pain and grief for each and every particle of truth that he had imparted to the ignorant and the humble!

Marc, who stood on the threshold of the house, dizzy with happiness, watching that triumph approach amid an explosion of fraternity and affection, bethought himself of the far-off day of Simon's arrest, the hateful day when a vehicle had carried him away from Maillebois at the moment of little Zéphirin's funeral. A furious crowd had rushed to seize him, roll him in the mud, and tear him to pieces. A horrible clamour had arisen: 'To death, to death with the assassin and sacrilegist! To death, to death with the Jew!' And the crowd had pursued the rolling wheels, unwilling to relinquish its prey, while Simon, pale and frozen, responded with his ceaseless cry: 'I am innocent! I am innocent! I am innocent!' And now that after long years that innocence was manifest, how striking was the transformation! The crowd was rejuvenated, transfigured; the children and the grandchildren of the blind insulters of former days had grown up in knowledge of truth, and become enthusiastic applauders, striving by dint of sincerity and affection to redeem the crime of their forerunners!

But the landau drew up before the garden gate, and the emotion increased when Simon was seen to alight with the help of his brother David, who had remained more nimble and vigorous. Emaciated, reduced to a shadow, Simon had white hair and a gentle countenance, softened by extreme age. He smiled his thanks to David, and again there were frantic acclamations at the sight of those two brothers, bound together by long years of heroism. The cheers continued when, after the Mayor, Jules Savin, Delbos also alighted—the great Delbos, as the crowd called him, the hero of Beaumont and Rozan, who had not feared to speak the truth aloud in the terrible days when it was perilous to do so, and who ever since had worked for the advent of a just society. Then, as Marc went forward to meet Simon and David, whom Delbos had just joined, the four men found themselves together for a moment on the very threshold of the house. And at that sight there came an increase of enthusiasm. Cries were raised and arms were waved deliriously as the three heroic defenders and the innocent man, whom they had rescued from the worst of tortures, were seen thus standing side by side.

Then Simon impulsively cast himself on the neck of Marc, who returned his embrace. Both sobbed, and were only able to stammer a few words—almost the same as they had stammered long ago, on the abominable day when they had been parted.

'Thank you, thank you, comrade. Like David, you have been to me a brother—a second brother; you saved my own and my children's honour.'

'Oh! I merely helped David, comrade; the victory was won by truth alone.... And there are your children—of their own accord they have grown up in strength and reason.'

The whole family, indeed, was assembled amid the garden greenery; four generations awaited the venerable old man, who triumphed after so many years of suffering. Rachel, his wife, stood beside Geneviève, the wife of his dear, good friend. Then came those whose blood had mingled—Joseph and Louise, Sarah and Sébastien, accompanied by their children, François and Thérèse, who were followed by little Rose, the last born of the line. Clément and Charlotte were also present with Lucienne. And tears started from all eyes, and endless kisses were exchanged.

But a very fresh, sweet song arose. The children of the boys' and girls' schools, the pupils of Joseph and Louise, were singing a welcome to the former schoolmaster of Maillebois. Nothing could have been more simple and more touching than that childish strophe, instinct with tenderness and suggestive of the happy future. Then a lad stepped forward and offered Simon a bouquet in the name of the boys' school.

'Thank you, my little friend. How fine you look.... Who are you?'

'I am Edmond Doloir; my father is Léon Doloir, a schoolmaster; he is yonder, beside Monsieur Salvan.'

Then came the turn of a little girl, who, in like fashion, carried a bouquet offered by the girls' school.

'Oh! what a pretty little darling! Thank you, thank you.... And what is your name?'

'I am Georgette Doloir; I am the daughter of Adrien Doloir and Claire Bongard. You can see them there with my grandpapa and grandmamma, and my uncles and aunts.'

But there was yet another bouquet, and this was presented by Lucienne Froment on behalf of Rose Simon, the last-born of the family, whom she carried in her arms. And Lucienne recited: 'I am Lucienne Froment, the daughter of Clément Froment and Charlotte Savin.... And this is Rose Simon, the little daughter of your grandson François, and your own great-granddaughter, as she is also the great-granddaughter of your friend Marc Froment through her grandmother, Louise.'

With trembling hands Simon took the dear and bonnie babe in his arms. 'Ah! you dear little treasure, flesh of my flesh, you are like the ark of alliance.... Ah, how good and vigorous has life proved! how bravely it has worked in giving us so many strong, healthy, and handsome offspring! And how everything broadens at each fresh generation; what an increase of truth and justice and peace does life bring as it pursues its eternal task!'

They were now all pressing around him, introducing themselves, embracing him, and shaking his hands. There were the Savins, Jules and his son Robert, the former the Mayor who had so actively helped on the work of reparation, and who had received him at the railway station on behalf of the whole town. There were the Doloirs also—Auguste, who had built the house, Adrien, who had planned it, Charles, who had undertaken the locksmith's work, and Marcel, who had attended to the carpentry. There were likewise the Bongards—Fernand and his wife Lucille, and Claire their daughter. And all were mingled, connected by marriages, forming, as it were, but one great family, in such wise that Simon could hardly tell who was who. But his old pupils gave their names, and he traced on their aged faces some likeness to the boyish features of long ago, while embrace followed embrace amid ever-increasing emotion. And all at once, finding himself in presence of Salvan, now very old indeed, but still showing a smiling countenance, Simon fell into his arms, saying, 'Ah! my master, I owe everything to you; it is your work which now triumphs, thanks to the valiant artisans of truth whom you formed and sent out into the world!'

Then came the turn of Mademoiselle Mazeline, whom he kissed gaily on both cheeks, and next that of Mignot, who shed tears when Simon had embraced him.

'Have you forgiven me, Monsieur Simon?' he asked.

'Forgiven you, my old friend Mignot! You have shown a valiant and noble heart! Ah! how delightful it is to meet again like this!'

The ceremony, so simple, yet so grand, was at last drawing to a close. The house offered to the innocent man, that bright-looking house standing on the site of the old den of the Rue du Trou, smiled right gaily in the sunlight with its decorative garlands of flowers and foliage. And all at once the drapery which still hung before the inscription above the door was pulled aside, and the marble slab appeared with its inscription in vivid letters of gold: 'Presented by the town of Maillebois to Schoolmaster Simon in the name of Truth and Justice, and as Reparation for the Torture inflicted on him.' Then came the signature, which seemed to show forth in a yet brighter blaze: 'The Grandchildren of his Persecutors.' And at that sight, from all the great square, and from the neighbouring avenue, from every window and from every roof, there arose a last mighty acclamation, which rolled on like thunder—an acclamation in which all at last united, none henceforth daring to deny that truth and justice had triumphed.

On the morrow *Le Petit Beaumontais* published an enthusiastic account of the ceremony. That once filthy print had been quite transformed by the new spirit, which had raised its readers both morally and intellectually. Its offices, so long infected by poison, had been swept and purged. The Press will, indeed, become a most admirable instrument of education when it is no longer, as now, in the hands of political and financial bandits, bent on debasing and plundering their readers. And thus *Le Petit Beaumontais,* cleansed and rejuvenated, was beginning to render great services, contributing day by day to increase of enlightenment, reason, and brotherliness.

A few days later a terrible storm, one of those September storms which consume everything, destroyed the Capuchin chapel at Maillebois. That chapel was the last religious edifice of the district remaining open, and several bigots still attended it. At Jonville, Abbé Cognasse had lately been found dead in his sacristy, carried off by an apoplectic stroke, which had followed one of his violent fits of anger; and his church, long empty, was now definitively closed. At Maillebois, Abbé Coquard no longer even opened the doors of St. Martin's, but officiated alone at the altar, unable as he was to find a server for the Mass. Thus the little chapel of the Capuchins, which, with its big gilded and painted statue of St. Antony of Padua, standing amid candles and artificial flowers, retained to the end its reputation as a miracle-shop, sufficed for the few folk who still followed the observances of the Church.

That day, as it happened, they were celebrating there some festival connected with the saint,[3] a ceremony which had attracted about a hundred of the faithful. Yielding to the solicitations of Father Théodose, Father Crabot, who nowadays remained shut up at La Désirade, where he intended to install some pious enterprise, had decided to honour the solemnity with his presence. Thus both were there, one officiating, the other seated in a velvet arm-chair before the statue of the great saint, who was implored to show his miraculous power and obtain from God the grace of some dreadful cataclysm, such as would at once sweep away the infamous and sacrilegious society of the new times. And it was then that the storm burst forth. A great inky, terrifying cloud spread over Maillebois; there came flashes of lightning, which seemed to show the furnaces of hell blazing in the empyrean, and thunderclaps which suggested salvoes of some giant artillery bombarding the earth. Father Théodose had ordered the bells to be rung, and a loud and prolonged pealing arose from the chapel, as if to indicate to the Deity that this was His house and should be protected by Him. But in lieu thereof extermination came. A frightful clap resounded, the lightning struck the bells, descended by the rope, and burst forth in the nave with a detonation as if the very heavens were crumbling. Father Théodose, fired as he stood at the altar, flamed there like a torch. The sacerdotal vestments, the sacred vases, the very tabernacle, were melted, reduced to ashes. And the great St. Antony, shivered to pieces, fell upon the stricken Father Crabot, of whom only a bent and blackened skeleton remained beneath all the dust. And as if those two ministers of the Church were not sufficient sacrifice, five of the devotees present were also killed, while the others fled, howling with terror, eager to escape being crushed by the vaulted roof, which cracked, then crumbled in a pile of remnants, leaving nought of the cult intact.

> [3] The real festival of St. Antony of Padua falls on June 13th.—*Trans.*

The stupefaction was universal throughout Maillebois. How could the Deity of the Holy Roman and Apostolic Church have made such a mistake? The same question had often been asked in former times—each time, indeed, that a church had been struck and its steeple had fallen on the priest and the kneeling worshippers. Had God desired, then, the end of the religion which had taken His name? Or, more reasonably, was it that no Divine hand whatever guided the lightning, and that it was but a natural force, which would prove a source of happiness whenever mankind should have domesticated it? In any case, after the calamity, Brother Gorgias suddenly reappeared and was seen hurrying along the streets of Maillebois, crying aloud that God had made no mistake. It was to him, he said, that God had hearkened, resolving to strike down his imbecile and cowardly superiors, and thus give a lesson to the whole Church, which could only flourish anew by the power of fire and steel. And a month later Gorgias himself was found, his skull split, his body soiled with filth, outside the same suspicious house before which, some time previously, a passer had already found the body of Victor Milhomme.

CHAPTER IV

Years, and again years, elapsed, and, thanks to the generosity of life,—which, as Marc had lived and served it so well, wished, it seemed, to reward him by keeping him and his adored Geneviève erect like triumphant spectators,—he, now over eighty, still tasted the supreme joy of seeing his dreams fulfilled yet more and more.

Generations continued to arise, each more freed, more purified, more endowed with knowledge than its forerunners. In former days there had been two Frances, each receiving a different education, remaining ignorant of the other, hating it, and contending with it. For the multitude of the nation, for the immense majority of the country folk, there had only been what was called elementary instruction—reading, writing, a little arithmetic, the rudiments which raised man just a span above the level of the brute beast. To the *bourgeoisie,* the petty minority of the elect, who had seized all wealth and power, secondary education and superior education, every means of learning and reigning, lay open. Thus was perpetuated the most frightful of all social iniquities. The poor and the humble were kept down in their ignorance beneath a heavy tombstone. To them it was forbidden to learn, to become men of knowledge, power, and mastery. At rare intervals one of them escaped and raised himself to the highest rank. But that was the exception, tolerated, and cited with canting hypocrisy as an example. All men were equal, it was said, and might raise themselves by their own merits. But as a first step, by way of preventing it, the necessary instruction, the enlightenment due to each and every child of the nation, was withheld from the great majority, so intense, indeed, was the terror of the great movement of truth and justice which would accrue from the diffusion of knowledge—a movement which would sweep away the *bourgeoisie* and its monstrous errors and compel disgorgement of the national fortune, in order that by just labour the city of solidarity and peace might be at last established.

And now a France which soon would be all one was being constituted; there would soon be no upper class, no lower class; those who knew would cease to crush and exploit those who did not know in a stealthy, fratricidal warfare, whose paroxysms had often reddened the paving of the streets with blood. A system of integral education for one and all was already at work; all the children of France had to pass through the gratuitous, secular, compulsory primary schools, where experimental facts, in lieu of grammatical rules, were now the bases of all education. Moreover, the acquirement of knowledge did not suffice; it was necessary one should learn to love, for it was only by love that truth could prove fruitful. And a process of natural selection ensued according to the tastes, aptitudes, and faculties of the pupils, who from the primary schools passed to special schools, arranged in accordance with requirements, embracing all practical applications of knowledge and extending to the highest speculations of the human mind. The law was that no member of a nation was privileged; that each being born into the world was to be welcomed as a possible force, whose culture was demanded by the national interests. And in this there was not only equality and equity, but a wise employment of the common treasure, a practical desire to lose nought that might contribute to the power and grandeur of the country. And, indeed, what a mighty awakening there was of all the accumulated energy which had lain slumbering in the country districts and the industrial towns! Quite an intellectual florescence sprang up, a new generation, able to act and think, supplying the sap which had long been exhausted in the old governing classes, worn out by the abuse of power. Genius arose daily from the fertile popular soil; a great epoch, a renascence of mankind, was impending. Integral instruction, which the ruling *bourgeoisie* had so long opposed, because it felt that it would destroy the old social order, was, indeed, destroying it, but at the same time it was setting in its place the fresh and magnificent blossoming of all the intellectual and moral power which would make France the liberator, the emancipator of the world.

Thus disappeared the divided France of former times, the France in which there had been two classes, two hostile, ever-warring races, reared, it might have been thought, in different planets, as if they were destined never to meet, never to come to an agreement. The schoolmasters, also, were no longer herded in two unfriendly groups, the one full of humiliation, the other full of contempt—on one side the poor, imperfectly educated elementary teachers, scarcely cleansed of the loam of their native fields, and on the other the professors of the Lycées and the special schools, redolent of science and literature. The masters who now taught the pupils of the primary schools followed them through all the stages of their education. It was held that a man needed as much intelligence and training to be able to awaken a boy's mind, impart first principles, and set him on the right road, as to maintain him in it and develop his faculties subsequently. A rotatory service was organised, teachers were easily recruited, and worked right zealously now that the profession had become one of the first of the land, well paid, honoured, and glorified.

The nation had also understood it to be necessary that the integral instruction it imparted should be gratuitous at all stages, however great might be the cost, for its millions were not cast stupidly to the winds, to foster falsehood and slaughter—they helped to rear good artisans of prosperity and peace. No other harvest could be compared with that: each *sou* that was expended helped to give more intelligence and strength to the people, helped it to master to-morrow. And the inanity of the great reproach levelled at the general diffusion of knowledge, that of casting *déclassés*, rebels, across the narrow limits of old-time society, became plainly manifest now that those limits had crumbled as the new society came into being. The *bourgeoisie*, even as it feared, was bound to be swept away as soon as it no longer possessed a monopoly of knowledge. But if in former years each penniless and hungry peasant's or artisan's son who rose up by the acquirement of knowledge had become a source of embarrassment and danger by reason of his eagerness to carve for himself a share of enjoyment among that of those who enjoyed already, that danger had now disappeared. There could be no more *déclassés*, since the classes themselves had ceased to exist, and no more rebels either, since the normal condition of life was the ascent of one and all towards more and more culture, in order that the most useful civic action might ensue. Thus education had accomplished its revolutionary work, and it was now the very strength of the community, the power which had both broadened and tightened the bond of brotherliness, all being called upon to work for the happiness of all, the energy of none remaining ignored and lost.

That complete education, the culture of the whole community, which now yielded such a magnificent harvest, had only become possible on the day when the Church had been deprived of her teaching privileges. The separation of Church and State, and the suppression of the budget of Public Worship, had freed the country and enabled it to dower its schools more liberally. The priest ceased to be a functionary, the Catholic faith no longer possessed the force of a law; those who chose remained free to go to church, even as to the theatre, by paying for their seats, but, in the result, the churches gradually emptied. And if this occurred it was because they no longer manufactured worshippers, poor stupefied beings, such as they needed to fill their naves. Long and terrible years had elapsed before it had become possible to wrest the children from the teachers of the Church, those who had poisoned mankind through the ages, who had reigned over it by falsehood and terrorism. From the very first day the Church had realised that she must kill truth if she did not wish it to kill her; and what furious battles had followed, what a desperate resistance she had offered in order to delay her inevitable defeat, the resplendent outpouring of Light, freed at last from every hindrance! Society would soon be reduced to treating her as one treated those malodorous fishwives whose shops were closed by the police. Yet she, the dogmatic and authoritarian ruler—she who, imitating her Deity, strove to impose her will on the world by thunderbolts, impudently dared to invoke and claim liberty, in order that she might perpetuate her abominable work of debasement and servitude. Laws of social protection then proved necessary; it became imperative to deprive her legally of her power, by refusing to her members, the monks and the priests, the right of teaching. And then again what an uproar followed, what frantic attempts to plunge France into civil war, credulous parents being banded together, while the religious orders, thrust out by the doorways once more, slipped into their dens by the windows, with the obstinacy of folk who relied on the eternal credulity which they fancied they had sown in the minds of men! Did they not represent error, superstition, and wretched human cowardice, and did it not follow, therefore, that eternity was theirs? But, for this to be, they had to retain their hold upon the children, and, by them, obscure the morrow; and it happened that the morrow and the children gradually escaped them, and that the time came when the Holy Roman Catholic Church lay agonising beneath the crumbling of her idiotic dogmas, pierced and destroyed by science. Truth had conquered, the schools given to all had formed men who knew, and who could exercise their will.

Thus hardly a day elapsed without Marc observing some fresh fortunate conquest, some increase of reason and comfort. He and his wife Geneviève alone remained erect of all the valiant generation which had fought and suffered so much. Good old Salvan had been the first to depart, then Mademoiselle Mazeline and Mignot had followed him. But of all the deaths the most painful for Marc had been those of Simon and David, the two brothers, carried off one after the other at an interval of only a few days, as if they had been still linked together by their heroic fraternity. Madame Simon had preceded them; all who had participated in the monstrous affair were now beneath the peaceful soil, lying there side by side, the good and the wicked, the heroes and the criminals, all plunged in eternal silence. Many of the children and grandchildren, moreover, had departed before their parents, for death never paused in his mysterious work, mowing down men as he listed in order to fertilise one or another field, whence other men would spring.

At last, quitting their retreat of Jonville, Marc and Geneviève had come to reside again at Maillebois, where they occupied the first floor of the house presented to Simon, and now belonging to his children, Joseph and Sarah. She and her husband Sébastien still resided at Beaumont, where the latter remained director of the Training College. But Joseph, afflicted in the legs, almost infirm, had been obliged to retire; and as his wife Louise had at the same time quitted the Maillebois school, they were now installed on the second floor of the paternal house, which the family shared in this fashion, well pleased to be together during the last gentle, declining days of life. And if they themselves had given up teaching, they at least had the joy of seeing the good work carried on by their descendants, for François and Thérèse had now been appointed to the Maillebois schools, in which, therefore, three generations of the family had succeeded one another.

The delight of living side by side, in close affection, had lasted two years, when quite a drama plunged the family into grief. One of those insensate passions which devastate a man came upon François, then in all the strength of his two and thirty years, and hitherto so tenderly attached to his wife Thérèse. He became enamoured of a young woman of eight and twenty years named Colette Roudille, whose mother, a very pious widow, had lately died. Colette's father was said to have been Théodose, the Capuchin, at one time her mother's confessor; and she certainly resembled him, having a splendid head, with blood-red lips and eyes of fire. The widow had lived on a little income, upon which, however, her son Faustin, twelve years older than his sister, had encroached to such a degree that the old woman had remained at last with barely enough money to buy bread. However, the little clerical group, all that remained of the once powerful faction which had ruled the district, took an interest in Faustin, and ended by obtaining a situation for him. For some months, then, he had been keeper of the estate of La Désirade, which since Father Crabot's death had become the subject of a number of lawsuits, and which some of the neighbouring localities proposed to purchase and turn into a people's palace and convalescent home, even as Valmarie had been turned into an asylum where young mothers recovered their strength. Thus Colette lived alone and in all freedom at Maillebois, almost in front of the school; and it was certain that the glow of her fine eyes and the smile of her red lips had largely helped on the passion which was maddening François.

But it happened that one day Thérèse surprised them, and dolorous anger came upon her, the more particularly as she was not the only one who might suffer from her husband's folly. Might it not, indeed, prove a disaster for their daughter Rose, who was now near her twelfth birthday? At one moment Thérèse appealed to her parents, Sébastien and Sarah, wishing to have their views respecting the course she ought to take. She spoke of a separation, offering to restore freedom to the husband who had ceased to love her and who told her lies. But she remained very calm, firm, and sensible in her trouble, and she soon understood that on this occasion it was wise and fit to forgive. Moreover, Marc and Geneviève, afflicted by the rupture, lectured their grandson François severely, and he evinced great sorrow, recognising that he was in the wrong, and accepting the most violent reproaches. But even while he confessed his fault, he unhappily remained disturbed, full of anguish, with an evident fear that his passion might again overcome him. Never had Marc so cruelly realised the fragility of human happiness. It was not sufficient, then, that one should instruct men and lead them towards justice by the paths of truth; it was also necessary that passion should not rend them and cast them one against the other like madmen. Marc had spent his life fighting in order that a little light might extricate the children from the dim gaol in which their fathers had groaned; and, in giving more happiness to others, he thought he had given it to his own family. Yet now, at the hearth of his grandson, who had seemed quite freed from error and very sensible, another form of suffering displayed itself—the suffering of love, with its eternal felicity and eternal torture! It was evident that one must not be proud of one's knowledge, that one must not set all one's strength in it. It was necessary that one should also be prepared to suffer in one's heart, and strive to make it valiant in order that it might bear up against a rending which always remained possible. And, again, it was wrong to think that it was sufficient to do good in order to be sheltered from the blows of evil. But though Marc said all those things to himself, placing a very modest estimate on the work he had accomplished, he still felt very sad as he saw mankind voluntarily leaving some of its flesh on all the briars of its path, and lingering there, as if unwilling to reach the happy city.

The holidays arrived, and all at once François disappeared. It seemed as if he had waited to be rid of his pupils in order to go off with Colette, the shutters of whose windows facing the High street remained closed. Wishing to stifle the scandal, the family related that, as François was in poor health, he had gone with a friend to take an air cure abroad during the holidays. A tacit understanding ensued in Maillebois—everybody pretended to accept that explanation out of regard for Thérèse, the forsaken wife, who was much liked and respected; but nobody really remained ignorant of the true cause of her husband's flight. She behaved admirably in those painful circumstances, hiding her tears, preserving perfect dignity in her home. In particular she bestowed increased tenderness on her daughter Rose, from whom, unfortunately, she could not hide the facts, but in whom she inculcated a continuance of respect for her father in spite of his bad conduct.

A month went by, and Marc, who was deeply grieved, still visited Thérèse every day, when one evening there came a dramatic, a horrible, occurrence. Rose having gone to spend the afternoon with a little friend in the neighbourhood, Marc had found Thérèse alone, sobbing in silence, far away from all prying eyes. For a long while he strove to comfort her and restore her to some hope. Then, at nightfall, he was obliged to leave her without having seen Rose, who had remained apparently with her little friend. The evening was dark, the atmosphere heavy with a threatening storm, and as Marc, eager to get home, was crossing the small, dim square behind the school, into which looked the window of the room once occupied by little Zéphirin, he suddenly heard a confused noise of footsteps and calls.

'What is the matter? What is the matter?' he exclaimed as he went forward.

He felt a chill in his veins, though why it was he could not tell. Apparently some gust of terror, coming from afar, was sweeping by. And at last in the faint light Marc perceived a man whom he recognised as a certain Marsouillier, a poor nephew of the deceased Philis, at one time mayor of Maillebois. Marsouillier now acted as beadle at St. Martin's, where, since the destruction of the Capuchin Chapel, a small party of believers still supported a priest.

'What is the matter?' Marc repeated, surprised to see that the other was gesticulating and mumbling to himself.

Marsouillier in his turn now recognised Marc. 'I don't know, Monsieur Froment,' he stammered with a terrified air. 'I was passing; I had come from the Place des Capucins, when, all at once, I heard the cries of a child, choking, it seemed, with fright. And as I hastened up I just caught sight of a man running away, while yonder on the ground lay that little body.... Then I also began to call.'

Marc himself now distinguished a pale and motionless form lying on the ground. And a suspicion came to him, Was it this man Marsouillier who had ill-used the child? Perhaps so, for curiously enough he was holding something white—a handkerchief.

'And that handkerchief?' Marc asked.

'Oh! I picked it up here just now.... Perhaps the man wanted to stifle the child's cries with it, and dropped it as he ran away.'

But Marc no longer listened; he was leaning over the little form upon the ground, and an exclamation of frantic grief suddenly escaped his lips: 'Rose! our little Rose!'

The victim was indeed the pretty little girl, who, as a babe, in the arms of her cousin Lucienne, had offered a bouquet to Simon on the occasion of his triumph ten years previously. She had grown up full of beauty and charm, with a bright, dimpled, smiling face amid a mass of fair and wavy tresses. And the scene could be easily pictured: the child returning home across that deserted square in the falling night, some bandit surprising her, ill-using her, and flinging her there upon the ground, whereupon, hearing a sound of footsteps, he had been seized with terror and had fled. The child did not stir; she lay there as if lifeless, in her little white frock figured with pink flowerets, a holiday frock which her mother had allowed her to wear for her visit to her friend.

'Rose! Rose!' called Marc, who was beside himself. 'Why do you not answer me, my darling? Speak, say only one word to me, only one word.'

He touched her gently, not daring as yet to raise her from the ground. And, talking to himself, he said, 'She has only fainted; I can tell that she is breathing. But I fear that something is broken.... Ah! misfortune dogs us; here again is grief indeed!'

Indescribable terror came upon him as all the frightful past suddenly arose before his mind's eye. There, under that tragic window, close to that room where the wretched Gorgias had killed little Zéphirin, he had now found his own great-granddaughter, his well-loved little Rose, who was assuredly hurt, and who in all probability only owed her salvation to the accidental arrival of a stranger. Who was it that had brought about that awful renewal of the past? What new and prolonged anguish was foreboded by that crime? As if by the glow of a great lightning flash, Marc, at that horrible moment, saw all his past life spread out, and lived all his battles and all his sufferings anew.

Marsouillier, however, had remained there with the handkerchief in his hand. He ended by slipping it into his pocket in an embarrassed way, like a man who had not said all he knew, and who devoutly wished that he had not crossed the square that evening.

'One ought not to leave her there, Monsieur Froment,' he said at last. 'You are not strong enough to pick her up; if you like I will take her in my arms and carry her to her mamma's, as it is close by.'

Marc was compelled to accept the offer, and followed the sturdy beadle, who took the child up very gently, without rousing her from her fainting fit. In this wise they reached the mother's door, and for her what a shock it was when she beheld her well-loved child, now her only joy and comfort, brought back to her insensible, as pale as death in her bright frock, and with her beautiful hair streaming loosely about her! The frock was in shreds, a lock of hair which had been torn off was caught in the lace collar. And the struggle must have been terrible, for the child's wrenched hands were all bruised, and her right arm hung down so limply that it was certainly broken.

Thérèse, distracted, beside herself, repeated amid her choking sobs: 'Rose, my little Rose! They have killed my Rose!'

In vain did Marc point out to her that the child was still breathing, and that not a drop of blood was to be seen; the mother still repeated that her child was dead. But Marsouillier carried the girl upstairs and laid her on a bed, where all at once she suddenly opened her eyes and gazed around her with indescribable terror. Then, shivering the while, she began to stammer: 'Oh, mamma, mamma, hide me, I am frightened!'

Thunderstruck by her revival to consciousness, Thérèse sank on the bed beside her, caught her in her arms and pressed her to her bosom, so overcome by emotion that she could no longer speak. Marc, however, begged the assistant teacher, who happened to be present, to go for a doctor; and then, quite upset by the mystery, endeavoured to fathom it at once.

'What happened to you, my darling?' he inquired; 'can you tell us?'

Rose looked at him for a moment as if to make sure who was speaking to her, and then, with haggard, wandering eyes, peered into all the dim corners of the room. I'm afraid, I'm afraid, grandfather,' she said.

He endeavoured to reassure her and inquired gently: 'Did nobody accompany you when you left your little friend's?'

'I didn't want anybody to come. The house is so near. And we had played so long, I was afraid I would get home still later.'

'And so you came back running, my darling, eh? And somebody sprang on you; that is what happened, is it not?'

But the terrified child again began to tremble, and did not answer. Marc had to repeat his question. 'Yes, yes, somebody,' she stammered at last.

Marc waited till she became calmer, caressing her hair the while, and kissing her on the forehead. 'You see, you ought to tell us,' he resumed. 'You cried out, naturally, you struggled. The man wanted to close your mouth, did he not?'

'Oh, grandfather, it was all so quick! He took hold of my arms, and he twisted them round. He wanted to drive me out of my senses and carry me off on his back. It hurt me so dreadfully, I thought I should die, and I fell to the ground: that is all I remember.'

Marc felt greatly relieved; he was now convinced that nothing worse had happened, particularly as Marsouillier, on hearing the girl's cries, had hastened to the spot. And so he asked but one question more: 'And would you be able to recognise the man, my dear?'

Again Rose quivered, and her eyes became quite wild as if some terrible vision was rising before her. Then, covering her face with her hand, she relapsed into stubborn silence. As her glance had already fallen on Marsouillier and she had raised no exclamation on seeing him, Marc realised that he had been mistaken when he had suspected the beadle of the crime. Nevertheless he wished to question him also; for, even allowing that he had spoken the truth, it might be that he had not told the whole of it.

'You saw the man run away?' said Marc. 'Would you be able to recognise him?'

'Oh! I don't think so, Monsieur Froment. He passed me, but it was already dark. Besides, I was so disturbed.' And the beadle, who had not yet fully recovered his composure, let a further detail escape him: 'He said something as he passed, I fancy ... he called "Imbecile!"'

'What! Imbecile?' retorted Marc, who was greatly surprised. 'Why should he have said that to you?'

But Marsouillier, deeply regretting that he had added that particular, for he understood the possible gravity of any admission on his part, endeavoured to recall his words. 'I can't be sure of anything,' he said, 'it was like a growl.... And no, no, I should not be able to recognise him.'

Then, as Marc asked him for the handkerchief, he drew it from his pocket with some appearance of *ennui*, and laid it on a table. It was a very common kind of handkerchief, one of those which are embroidered by the gross with initials in red thread. This one was marked with the letter F, and the clue was a slight one, for dozens of similar handkerchiefs were sold in the shops.

Meantime Thérèse, who had again caught Rose in a gentle embrace, caressed her lovingly. 'The doctor is coming, my treasure,' she said. 'I won't touch you any more till he is here. It won't be anything. You are not in great pain, are you?'

'No, mother,' Rose replied, 'but my arm burns me and seems very heavy.'

Then, in an undertone, Thérèse, in her turn, tried to confess the girl, for the mysteriousness of the assault had left her very anxious. But at each fresh question Rose evinced yet greater alarm, and at last she closed her eyes and buried her head in the pillow, so as to see and hear nothing more. Every time her mother made a fresh attempt, begging her to say if she knew the man and would be able to recognise him, the child quivered dreadfully. But all at once, bursting into loud sobs, quite beside herself, almost delirious, she told everything in a loud, distressful voice, fancying, perhaps, that she was simply whispering her words in her mother's ear.

'Oh! mother, mother, I am so grieved! I recognised him—it was father who was waiting there, and who threw himself upon me!'

Thérèse sprang to her feet in stupefaction. 'Your father? What is it you say, you unhappy child?'

Marc and Marsouillier also had heard the girl. And the former drew near to her with a violent gesture of incredulity: 'Your father? It is impossible!... Come, come, my darling, you must have dreamt that.'

'No, no, father was waiting for me behind the school, and I recognised him by his beard and his hat. He tried to carry me away, and as I would not let him he twisted my arms and made me fall.'

She clung stubbornly to that account of the affair, though she could supply little proof of what she asserted, for the man had not spoken a word to her, and she had only noticed his beard and hat, remembering nothing else, not even his features, which had been hidden by the darkness. Nevertheless, that man was her father, she was sure of it; nothing could efface that impression, which, if incorrect, might be some haunting idea which had sprung from the grief in which she had seen her mother plunged since the departure of the unfaithful François.

'It is impossible; it is madness!' Marc repeated, for his reason rebelled and protested against such a notion. 'If François had wished to take Rose away he would not have hurt her—killed her almost!'

Thérèse also quietly displayed a feeling of perfect certainty. 'François is incapable of such an action,' said she. 'He has caused me a great deal of grief, but I know him, and will defend him if need be.... You were mistaken, my poor Rose.'

Nevertheless the unhappy woman went to look at the handkerchief which had remained on the table. And she could not restrain a nervous start, for it appeared to be one of a dozen marked with a similar letter F, which she had purchased for her husband of the sisters Landois, who kept a drapery shop in the High Street. On going to a chest of drawers Thérèse found ten similar handkerchiefs, and it was quite possible that François had taken two away with him at the time of his flight. However, the unhappy wife strove to overcome her uneasiness, and as firmly and as positively as before, she said: 'The handkerchief may belong to him.... But it was not he; never shall I think him guilty.'

The strange scene seemed to have stupefied Marsouillier. He had remained on one side, at a loss apparently as to how he might quit those sorrowing folk, and since he had heard the child's story his eyes had been all astonishment. The recognition of the handkerchief brought his dismay to a climax, and at last, profiting by the arrival of the doctor fetched by the assistant teacher, he managed to slip away. Marc, on his side, went into the dining-room to await the result of the medical examination. Rose's right arm was indeed broken, but there was nothing of a disquieting character about the fracture, and the wrenched wrists and a few bruises were the only other marks of violence which the doctor found. He, indeed, was most concerned respecting the result of the nervous shock which the girl had experienced, for it had been a violent one. And he only left her an hour later, when he had reduced the fracture and saw her overcome, as it were, plunged in a heavy sleep.

Marc, however, had meantime sent a message to his wife and Louise, for he feared that they might be alarmed by his failure to return home. And they hastened to the school, terrified by this frightful business, which reminded them also of the old and abominable affair. Thérèse having joined them, a kind of family council was held, the door of the bedroom remaining open in order that they might at once hear the injured girl if she should wake up. Marc, who was quite feverish, expressed his views at length. What possible reason could there have been for François to commit such a deed? He might have yielded to a transport of passion by running away with Colette, but he had invariably shown himself to be a loving father, and his wife did not even complain of his manner towards herself, for it had remained outwardly dignified, almost deferential. Thus, what motive could have prompted him if he were guilty? Hidden away with his mistress in some unknown retreat, it could hardly be that he had experienced a sudden craving to have his daughter with him. What could he have done with the child? She would have been a burden on him in the life he must be leading. And even supposing that he had wished to strike a cruel blow at his wife, and reduce her to solitude, without a consolation remaining to her, it was incredible that he should have ill-used and injured his daughter, have left her upon the ground senseless! He would simply have taken her away with him. Thus, in spite of Rose's statements, in spite of the handkerchief, François could not be guilty, the impossibilities were too great. Nevertheless, faced as he was by this mysterious problem, and the task of again seeking the truth, Marc felt disturbed and anxious, for he was convinced that Marsouillier would relate what he had seen and heard, and that all Maillebois would be discussing the drama on the morrow. And as all the appearances were against François, would public opinion denounce him, even as in former days it had denounced his grandfather, Simon the Jew? In that case, how could he be defended? what ought to be done to prevent a renewal of the monstrous iniquity of long ago?

'The one thing that tends to tranquillise me,' said Marc at last, 'is that the times have changed. We now have to deal with people who have been freed and educated, and it will greatly surprise me if they do not help us to unravel the truth.'

Silence fell. At last, in spite of the little quiver which she was unable to master, Thérèse exclaimed energetically, 'You are right, grandfather. Before everything else we must establish the innocence of François, which I cannot possibly doubt, whatever may be the accusations.... He has made me suffer dreadfully, but I will forget it, and you may rely on me, I will help you with all my strength.'

Geneviève and Louise nodded their assent. 'Ah!' muttered the latter, 'the unhappy lad! When he was seven years old he used to throw his arms round me and say, "Little mother, I love you very dearly!" He has a tender and passionate nature, and thus one must forgive him a great deal.'

'There is always some resource when one has to deal with loving natures,' remarked Geneviève in her turn. 'Even if they become guilty of great transgressions, love helps them to repair them.'

On the morrow, even as Marc had foreseen, all Maillebois was in a hubbub. People talked of nothing but that assault, of the charge which the injured girl had brought against her own father, of the handkerchief picked up by a passer, and recognised by the wife. Marsouillier told the story to all who were willing to listen to him, and he even embellished it somewhat, making out that he had seen and done everything in connection with the rescue. He was not a malicious man, he was simply vain and inclined to poltroonery in such wise that while it flattered his feelings to become a personage he remained secretly apprehensive of great personal worries if the affair should turn out badly. He was, as already mentioned, a nephew of the pious Philis, and he lived on his pay as a beadle, which pay was extremely small now that only a few believers provided for the expenses at St. Martin's. And it was said that he himself was not a believer at all, that his views were really very free ones, and that if he thus ate the bread of hypocrisy it was simply because he was unable to earn any other. However that might be, the few remaining worshippers who paid his salary, the last Catholics of the district, who were enraged by their defeat and the abandonment into which the Church was sinking, at once seized upon his adventure and resolved to exploit that scandal which had assuredly been vouchsafed to them by Heaven. Never had they dared to hope for such an opportunity to resume hostilities, and they must profit by the divine favour to make a supreme effort. Thus black skirts were again seen gliding along the streets of Maillebois, old ladies were again heard telling the most extraordinary stories. Some unknown person had related that she had seen François on the night of the crime in the company of two masked men, who were Freemasons undoubtedly. And, as everybody knew that the Freemasons needed the blood of a young girl for their Black Mass, it followed that François, after some drawing of lots, had been chosen to provide the blood of his daughter. Did that not explain everything—the sectarian's savage violence, his unnatural ferocity? But it happened that the inventors of that idiotic fable could not find a single newspaper to print it, and thus they had to spread it by word of mouth among the poorer folk. When evening came it had already gone all round the town, and had even reached Jonville, Le Moreux, and other neighbouring villages. And the seed of falsehood being sown, the plotters only had to wait for the poisonous crop which they hoped to see arise from the popular ignorance.

But, as Marc had said, the times had changed. On all sides people shrugged their shoulders when they heard that foolish story. Such inventions had been all very well in former times, when men were children and fell eagerly on improbabilities. But nowadays people knew too much, and a story of that kind was not accepted without due examination. In the first place, it was immediately ascertained that François did not happen to be a Freemason. Moreover, nobody had seen him in the town; and it seemed certain that he was hidden away at a distance with that girl Colette, who had disappeared from Maillebois at the same time as himself. Again, there were all sorts of reasons for thinking him innocent. Indeed the whole district pronounced the same opinion on him as his relatives had done. He was a man of an amorous nature, who might yield to a passionate transport, but he was also a loving father, and as such incapable of ill-treating his own child. Excellent testimony came in from all sides. His pupils and their parents praised his gentleness; several neighbours related that in spite of his errors he had remained affectionately attached to his wife. Nevertheless, people were confronted by the accusations of Rose, the disquieting clue of the handkerchief, the scene repeatedly recounted by Marsouillier—the whole constituting an irritating mystery, a distressing problem for all who were competent to weigh and judge facts. If, indeed, François were not guilty, however much appearances might be against him, somebody else must be the culprit, and who could that be, and how was he to be discovered?

Then, while the judicial authorities were inquiring into the matter, something quite new was seen—mere ordinary townsfolk came forward, quite voluntarily, to relate whatever they knew, whatever they had witnessed, felt, or surmised. Now that men's minds were cultivated there was a general desire for justice, a dread of any possible error. A Bongard came to say that on the evening of the assault, while he was passing the town hall, he had seen a man who looked somewhat scared, and who seemed to have run up from the direction of the Place des Capucins. And that man was not François. Then a Doloir brought a smoker's tinder-box, which he had found between two paving-stones behind the schools. And he pointed out that this box might have fallen from the culprit's pocket, and that François did not smoke. A Savin also recounted that he had overheard a conversation between two old ladies, from which he had drawn the conclusion that the culprit was to be sought among the acquaintances of Marsouillier, the latter having let his tongue wag while he was in the company of certain friendly devotees. But the most intelligent and active helpers were the sisters Landois, who kept the drapery shop in the High Street. They had been pupils of Mademoiselle Mazeline; and, indeed, all the workers in the cause of truth, all the voluntary witnesses, had passed through the hands of the secular teachers, Marc, Joulic, or Joseph. As for the sisters Landois, it had occurred to them to consult their books to ascertain the names of the persons to whom they had sold handkerchiefs similar to the one which the culprit had wished to employ as a gag. They readily found François' name; and below it, two days later, they perceived that of Faustin Roudille, the brother of the young woman Colette, with whom François had fled. That was the first clue, the first gleam of the light which was to spread and become decisive.

As it happened, this man Faustin had been without a situation for the last fortnight. After coming to an agreement with the surrounding localities, the town of Maillebois had at last purchased the magnificent estate of La Désirade, which it intended to transform into a People's Palace, a convalescent home, a public park, open to all the workers of the region. Instead of some congregation of black frocks being installed in that delightful spot, under that royal verdure, among those plashing waters and those gleaming marbles, swains and their lassies, young mothers and their babes, old folk desirous of repose, would flock thither to enjoy the sweetness and splendour of the scene. Thus Faustin, the ex-keeper, a creature of the last remaining clericalists, had quitted the estate, and was to be seen prowling about Maillebois, showing himself very bitter and aggressive, especially with respect to his sister Colette, whose escapade, said he, had dishonoured him. People were somewhat surprised by this sudden severity on his part, for nobody was ignorant of the good understanding which had previously reigned between the brother and the sister, and the frequency with which the former had borrowed money from the young woman when he knew her to be in funds. Had there been a rupture, then? Was Faustin exasperated with Colette because she had taken herself off just as he lost his situation? Or was he playing some comedy, still remaining in agreement with his sister, acquainted with her hiding-place, and secretly working on her behalf? These points remained obscure, but the discovery made by the sisters Landois directed general attention to Faustin, his actions, and his words. A week, then, sufficed for the inquiry to make considerable progress.

First of all, Bongard's evidence was confirmed; several people now remembered that on the evening of the assault they had met Faustin in the High Street, looking agitated, and turning round as if he wished to ascertain what might be taking place in the direction of the schools. And it was certainly he whom they had seen; they had positively recognised him. Then, too, the tinder-box found by Doloir seemed to belong to him—at least, folk asserted that they had seen a similar one in his hands. Finally, the conversation which Savin had overheard, and the hypothesis of an acquaintance between Marsouillier and the culprit received striking confirmation, for the beadle and the ex-keeper of La Désirade had been quite intimate. That seemed to be the decisive fact, the clue which would lead to full enlightenment, as Marc, who was following the inquiry with impassioned attention, immediately understood. Thus he took it upon himself to extract a confession from Marsouillier. He recalled the beadle's strange manner when he had found him near Rose after the culprit's flight. He remembered that he had seemed embarrassed and anxious, disturbed at having to give up the handkerchief; and he particularly recalled his stupefaction when Rose had accused her father, and Thérèse had produced some similar handkerchiefs from her chest of drawers. And he was greatly struck by that word 'Imbecile!' which the culprit had cast in the beadle's face, and which the latter in his perturbation had repeated. It was a significant word, it was like a reproach hurled by a man at a blundering friend whose inopportune arrival on the scene had spoilt everything.

Thus Marc called upon Marsouillier. 'You know, my man,' he said to him, 'the gravest charges are being accumulated against Faustin; he will certainly be arrested this evening. Are you not afraid of being compromised?'

Silent, with hanging head, the beadle listened to an enumeration of the proofs.

'Come, own that you recognised him!' Marc added.

'But how could I have recognised him, Monsieur Froment?' said Marsouillier. 'Faustin has no beard, and he wears a cap; whereas the man I saw had a full beard and a felt hat.'

Those were points which Rose herself confirmed, and which as yet remained unelucidated.

'Oh! he might have got a hat somewhere, and have put on a false beard,' Marc suggested. 'But in any case he spoke; you yourself told me so. Surely you must have recognised his voice when he called you an imbecile!'

Marsouillier was already raising his hand to contradict himself, and swear that the man had not pronounced a single word. But Marc's bright eyes were fixed upon him, and as he met their gaze his strength failed him. And then, good-hearted man as he was at bottom, he grew disturbed, no longer having the courage to do a bad action in some stupid spirit of vanity.

'Naturally I have inquired into your connection with Faustin,' Marc resumed. 'I know that you and he often met, and that he readily cast that expression "imbecile" in your face when he found you more scrupulous than he liked.'

'That's true,' Marsouillier admitted; 'he called me an imbecile, and it ended by being hardly pleasant.'

Then, on being pressed, exhorted to relieve his conscience in his own interest, for the authorities might believe him to be an accomplice, he ended by yielding to his fears as much as to his respect for truth. 'Well, yes, Monsieur Froment, I did recognise him.... Only he could have called me an imbecile in that voice. I can't be mistaken, he has given me that name too many times. And he must merely have worn a false beard, as you surmise, and have pulled it off as he ran away, for when some people saw him at the corner of the High Street he was wearing a hat, but he was shaven as usual, with no beard at all.'

Marc felt delighted, for this testimony would certainly prove decisive. Shaking hands with Marsouillier, he said to him: 'Ah! I knew it very well; you are a good fellow.'

'A good fellow, no doubt.... You see, Monsieur Froment, I am an old pupil of Monsieur Joulic, and when a master has taught one to love truth it never goes away. One may wish to tell a falsehood, but the whole of one's being rises up in protest. Besides, when one knows how to use one's reason a little, it becomes impossible to credit the foolish things which are put into circulation. I was very worried at heart about this unhappy affair. But then I'm a very poor man; I have only my post as beadle as a means of livelihood, and my position compelled me to say the same as the old friends of my uncle Philis.'

Then Marsouillier paused, and, with a gesture of despair, big tears gathering the while in his eyes, he added: 'Ah! I'm done for now. I shall be turned out of doors, and left to starve in the streets.'

But Marc reassured him by a positive promise to find him some employment. And then he hastened away, eager as he was to acquaint Thérèse with the result of the interview, that conclusive testimony by which François was completely cleared.

For a fortnight past Thérèse had remained nursing Rose, still feeling firmly convinced of her husband's innocence, but intensely hurt at receiving no news of him in spite of the stir occasioned by the affair, which all the newspapers had recounted. And since her daughter had been recovering, already able to get up, her arm healing in a satisfactory manner, Thérèse, mastered by increasing sorrow, had remained mute, quite overcome, in her deserted home. But that very evening, while Marc was gaily completing his account of his conversation with Marsouillier, she experienced a great shock, for François suddenly entered the room. And the scene was a poignant one, however simple might be the words that were exchanged.

'You did not think me guilty, Thérèse?'

'No, François, I assure you.'

'This morning, in the sad solitude in which I found myself, I was still ignorant of everything.... But I happened to glance at an old newspaper, and then I hastened here. How is Rose?'

'She is much better. She is there, in the bedroom.'

François had not dared to kiss his wife. She stood before him, erect and severe amid her emotion. But Marc, who had risen, caught hold of his grandson's hands, guessing by his pallor, his ravaged face, which still bore traces of his tears, that he had been involved in some tragic drama.

'Come, tell me everything, my poor lad.'

Then François, in a few quivering words and with all sincerity, recounted his folly—his sudden flight from Maillebois on the arm of that Colette who had maddened him; their life of seclusion in a lonely district of Beaumont, where they had scarcely quitted their room; a fortnight's cloistered life, interspersed with furious storms, extravagant caprices on the part of that passionate gipsy, reproaches, tears, and even blows; then, all at once, her flight nobody knew whither, after a last scene when she had flung the furniture at her lover's head. That had happened three weeks previously, and at first he had awaited her return, then buried himself, as it were, in the seclusion of that lonely room, full of despair and remorse, no longer knowing how to return to Maillebois to his wife, whom he declared he had never ceased to love in spite of all his folly.

While he spoke, Thérèse, who was still standing there, had turned her head aside. And when he had finished she said, 'There is no occasion for me to know those things.... I merely understand that you have come back to answer the charges brought against you.'

'Oh!' Marc gently observed, 'those charges have now ceased to exist.'

'I have come back to see Rose,' François on his side declared, 'and I repeat that I would have been here the very next day if I had not remained ignorant of everything.'

'Very good,' Thérèse rejoined; 'I do not prevent you from seeing your daughter; she is there—you may go in.'

There ensued a very singular scene which Marc watched with impassioned interest. Rose was seated in an armchair, reading, her injured arm hanging in a sling. As the door opened she looked up and raised a quivering cry, instinct, it seemed, both with fear and with joy.

'Oh! papa!'

Then she rose, and all at once seemed stupefied. 'But it wasn't you, papa—was it—the other evening?' she cried. 'The man was shorter and his beard was different!'

And she continued to scrutinise her father as if she found him otherwise than she had pictured him since his flight—since she had watched her forsaken mother weeping. Had she pictured him as a wicked man, then, squat of build and with an ogre's face? She now recognised the father with the pleasant smile, whom she adored; and if he had come back it was surely in order that no more tears might be shed in their dear home. But all at once she began to tremble at the thought of the dreadful consequences of her error.

'And to think I accused you, papa—that I kept on saying that the man was you! No, no, it wasn't you, I told a story; I will explain it to the gendarmes if they come to take you!'

She sank back in the arm-chair, weeping bitterly, and her father had to take her on his lap, kiss her, and vow to her that their sorrows were all over. He himself stammered with emotion as he spoke. Had he behaved so vilely, then, that he had appeared a very monster in the eyes of his daughter, and that she had thought him capable of ill-using her so dreadfully?

Thérèse, meantime, while listening, had striven to remain impassive, saying never a word. François glanced at her anxiously, as if to ascertain whether she would again tolerate his presence in that home which he had ravaged. And Marc, noticing the severity of her demeanour, her unwillingness to forgive, preferred to take his grandson away with him and provide him with a lodging pending the advent of a calmer hour.

That very evening the officers of the law presented themselves at Faustin's dwelling, but they did not find the rascal there. The place was closed, the man had fled, and the search for him failed: he was never taken. People ended by believing that he had escaped to America. His sister Colette had perhaps accompanied him thither, for although she was sought she was never seen again, either at Maillebois or at Beaumont. And the whole affair remained very obscure; one was reduced to conjectures. Had the brother and sister been accomplices? Had Colette co-operated in some plot when she had induced François to carry her off, or had Faustin merely wished to avail himself in some mysterious manner of the situation which the elopement had created? But the chief point of all was whether there had been some superior behind him, some man of intelligence and will, who had planned and prepared everything in view of a supreme assault on the new order of things, by renewing, as it were, the old Simon affair. All those suppositions were allowable, given the facts; and in the end nobody doubted that there had really been some mysterious agreement and ambush.

Thus, how great was Marc's relief when the authorities, being convinced of Faustin's guilt and flight, set the affair aside. At the first moment that renewal of the old abominations, that last supreme attempt to besmirch the secular schools, had greatly disquieted Marc. But he was astonished at the rapidity with which the truth had been made manifest by public good sense. The appearances against François had been far greater than those against Simon in the old days. His own daughter had accused him; and, even if she had retracted her words, it would simply have been said that she had yielded to family pressure. In former times no witnesses, neither a Bongard, nor a Doloir, nor a Savin, would have dared to come forward and say what they had heard or seen, for fear of compromising themselves. In former times Marsouillier would not have relieved his conscience; firstly, because he would have felt no need of doing so, and secondly because a powerful faction would have immediately risen to support and glorify his original falsehood. The Congregations had then been ready at hand, poisoning everything, making a dogma, a cult, of error. Rome in her battle against free thought had made a savage use of political parties, maddening them, hurling them one upon the other, in the hope of some civil war which, by cutting the nation in halves, might render her mistress of the majority, the poor and ignorant. And now that Rome was vanquished, that the Congregations were disappearing, that not a Jesuit would soon be left to obscure men's thoughts and pervert their actions, human reason was working freely. The explanation of all the good sense and logic which Marc had lately observed was not to be sought elsewhere. The simple fact was that the people, being now educated and freed from the errors of centuries, were becoming capable of truth and justice.

But amid the delight of victory some anxiety lingered in Marc's heart, anxiety at the rupture which had occurred between François and Thérèse, that question of the happiness of man and woman, which happiness can only spring from their perfect agreement. Marc did not entertain any wild hope of being able to kill the passions and prevent our poor humanity from bleeding beneath the spur of desire. There would always be broken hearts, tortured and jealous flesh. Only, might one not hope that woman, being freed and raised to equality with man, would render the sexual struggle less bitter, impart to it some calm dignity? Already during the recent scandal women had shown themselves the friends of truth, employing all their energy to discover it. They were emancipated from the Church; they were no longer possessed by base superstition and the fear of hell; they no longer feigned a false humility before the priests; they were no longer the servants who prostrated themselves before men, the sex which seems to acknowledge its abjection and which revenges itself for its enforced humility by rotting and disorganising everything. They had ceased to act as snares of voluptuousness in accordance with the discreet advice of their confessors, seeking to entrap men in order to promote the triumph of religion. They had become normal wives and mothers since they had been wrested from that morbid falsehood of the divine spouse, which had unhinged so many poor minds. And now was it not their duty to complete the great work by exercising the rights they had regained with great wisdom and kindness?

At last it occurred to Marc to assemble the whole family at the school, in that large classroom where he himself had taught, and where Joseph and François had taught after him. And there was a certain solemnity about that meeting, held one afternoon at the close of September, amid the sunshine which cast gentle beams on the master's desk, the boys' forms, the blackboards, and the pictures hanging from the walls. Sébastien and Sarah came from Beaumont; Clément and Charlotte arrived with their daughter Lucienne from Jonville. And Joseph, warned some days previously, had returned from a holiday tour feeling very much affected by all that had occurred in his absence. Finally, Marc himself and Geneviève, accompanied by Louise and Joseph, repaired to the rendezvous, taking François with them—Thérèse and Rose awaiting their arrival in the classroom. Altogether twelve members of the family attended the gathering, and at first deep silence prevailed.

'My dear Thérèse,' said Marc at last, 'we have no wish to do violence to your feelings, we have only come here for a family chat.... You have no doubt suffered in your heart, but you have never known such a great rending as when husband and wife have seemed to come from two different worlds, and have suddenly found themselves parted by such an abyss as to suggest no likelihood of ever being united again. In former times woman, in the hands of the Church, had become an instrument of torture for man, who was already freed. Ah! how many tears were shed in those days, how many homes were broken up!'

Silence fell again; then Geneviève, who was deeply moved, in her turn said: 'Yes, my dear Marc, I often regarded you wrongly, I often tortured you in the old days, and you do right to recall those evil years; your words cannot wound me now, since I have had strength enough to overcome the poison. But how many women remained agonising in the old dungeon, how many homes perished in grief? I myself have never been entirely cured; I have always trembled with the dread of being mastered once more by long heredity and the perverting influence of early education. And if I have managed to remain erect, it is thanks to you, your sturdy good sense and active affection, for all which I thank you, my good Marc.'

Happy tears had come into her eyes, and she continued with increasing emotion: 'Ah! my poor grandmother, my poor mother! Yes, they were to be pitied! They were so wretched, assailed by destructive ferments, cast out of their sex, as it were, by their voluntary martyrdom. My poor grandmother was a terrible woman; but then she had never known a joy in life, she lived in perpetual nothingness—and thus why should she not have dreamt of reducing others to the same painful renunciation of everything which she had imposed upon herself? And my poor mother, too, what a long agony did she undergo from having tasted the delight of being loved, and afterwards from having lapsed for ever into that religion of falsehood and death which denies all the powers and joys of life!'

While Geneviève spoke two shadowy forms seemed to flit by—the vanished forms of Madame Duparque and Madame Berthereau—those pitiable, disquieting devotees of another age, one of whom had belonged entirely to the ferocious, exterminating Church, while the other, of a gentler nature, had died in despair at the thought that she had never attempted to sever her chain. Geneviève's eyes seemed to wander away after them both. She herself had known the great battle, for it had been waged around her and within her; and it was happiness for her to think that she had one day felt free again, and had returned to life and to health. But her eyes at last fell upon her daughter Louise, who smiled at her very lovingly, and then leant forward to kiss her.

'Mother,' said Louise, 'you were the bravest and the most deserving, for it was you who fought and suffered. It is to you we owe the victory, paid for with so many tears. I remember. Coming as I did after you, it was no great merit for me to free myself from the past; and if never a quiver of error disturbed me, it was because I profited by the terrible lesson which at one time made all our hearts bleed in our poor mourning home.'

'Be quiet, you flatterer,' replied Geneviève, laughing and returning her kiss. 'You were the child who saved us, whose strong and skilful little mind intervened so lovingly and triumphed over every obstacle. We owe our peace to you; you were the first free little woman with enough intelligence, will, and resolution to set happiness on earth.

Then Marc, turning towards Thérèse, explained: 'You were not born, my dear, at the time of all those things, and you are ignorant of them. Having come after Louise, having never had anything to do with baptism or confession or communion, you find it easy and simple to live freely beyond the pale of religious imposture and social prejudice, with no other bonds about you than those of your own reason and conscience. But, for things to be as they are, mothers and grandmothers passed through frightful crises, the worst follies, the worst torments.... As is the case with all the social questions, the one solution lay in education. It was necessary to impart knowledge to woman before setting her in her legitimate place as the equal and companion of man. That was the first thing necessary, the essential condition of human happiness, for woman could only free man after being freed herself. As long as she remained the priest's servant and accomplice, an instrument of reaction, espionage, and warfare in the home, man himself remained in chains, incapable of all virile and decisive action. The strength of the future will lie in the absolute agreement of man and wife.... And so, my dear, you see how sad it makes us that misfortune should again have come into your home. There is no abyss created by different beliefs between you and François. You are of the same spheres, the same education. He is not your master by law and custom, as he would have been in the old days; you are not his servant, seeking an opportunity to revenge yourself on him for his mastery. You have the same rights as he has. You can dispose of your life as you choose. Your joint peace and agreement are based solely on reason, logic, and the dictates of life itself, which, to be lived in health and all fulness, requires the mating of man and woman. But, alas! we see your peace destroyed by the eternal fragility of human nature, unless indeed kindness of heart should help you to win it back.'

Thérèse had listened, calm, dignified, and with an expression of great deference: 'I know all those things, grandfather; you must not think I have forgotten them,' said she. 'But why has François been living with you for some days past? He might have remained here. There are two lodgings, the schoolmaster's and the schoolmistress's, and I do not prevent him from taking possession of the former while I occupy the other. In that fashion he can resume his duties when the boys come back in a few days' time. We are free, as you say, and I desire to remain free.'

Her father and her mother, Sébastien and Sarah, then tried to intervene affectionately; and Geneviève, Louise, and Charlotte, indeed all the women present, smiled at her, entreated her with their glances; but she would listen to nothing, she rejected their suggestions resolutely, though without any anger.

'François has wounded me cruelly,' she said. 'I thought I had quite ceased to love him, and I should be telling you a falsehood if I said that I am now certain I love him still.... You cannot wish me to tell an untruth, you cannot wish me to resume life in common with him, when it would be cowardice and shame.'

At this a cry escaped François, who hitherto had remained silent, and visibly anxious. 'But I, Thérèse, I still love you!' he exclaimed. 'I love you as I never loved you before, and if you have suffered, I think that I now suffer even more than you have done!'

She turned towards him, and said very gently:' You speak the truth, I am willing to believe it.... It is quite possible that you still love, in spite of your folly, for amid all our craving for reason, our poor human hearts will ever remain a source of dementia. And as you suffer so much, there are two of us who suffer ... dreadfully. But I cannot be your wife again if I no longer love you, if I no longer wish you for my husband. It would be unworthy of us both, our ill, in lieu of healing, would be poisoned by it. The best course for us to follow is to live as good neighbours, good friends, and attending to our work, each free once more.'

'But I, mamma!' cried Rose, whose eyes were full of tears.

'You, my darling? You will love us both to-morrow as you loved us yesterday.... And don't be anxious, these are questions which one only understands when one is older than you are.'

With a caressing gesture Marc summoned the girl to him, and, having seated her on his knees, he was about to plead the cause of François once more when Thérèse hastily forestalled him.

'No, no, grandfather, do not insist, I beg you. It is your tender heart, not your reason, that now wishes to speak. If you prevailed over me you might have cause to repent it. Let me be wise and strong.... I know very well that you wish to spare us suffering. Ah! let us confess that suffering will be eternal. It is in us, no doubt, for one of the unknown purposes of life. Our poor hearts will always bleed, we shall always rend them in hours of exasperated passion, in spite of all the health and all the good sense that we may succeed in acquiring. And, perhaps, that is the necessary good for happiness!'

A slight chilling quiver seemed to dim the bright sunlight; through all there passed a consciousness of the sorrowful grandeur of that recognition of suffering.

'But what does it matter?' Thérèse continued. 'Have no fears, grandfather, we will be worthy and brave. It is nothing to suffer, it is only necessary that suffering should not make us blind and wicked. Nobody will know that we suffer, and we will even try to be the better for it, more gentle to others, more desirous of assuaging the causes of grief which exist in the world.... And, besides, grandfather, do not regret anything; say to yourself that you have done all you possibly could do, that you have carried out an admirable task which will give us all the happiness that reason can yield. As for the rest, as for sentimental life, each with his or her love will settle that according to personal circumstances, even if it be in tears. Leave us, François and me, leave us to live and suffer even, as we choose, for it only concerns ourselves. It is sufficient that you should have freed our minds, and made us conscious of a world of truth and justice.... And as you have brought us together here, grandfather, it shall not be for the purpose of preventing a rupture, of which only François and myself can be the judges, but it shall be to give us an opportunity to acclaim you, to express to you our adoration, and our gratitude for your work!'

At this they all clapped hands, transported with delight, and the splendour of the sun seemed to have returned and to stream in a sheet of gold through the lofty windows. Yes, yes, this was the grandfather's triumph in that very classroom where he had fought so bravely, where he had given the best of his heart and his mind to those who would become the people of the morrow. Children, grandchildren, great-grandchildren, all were his pupils, and all surrounded him as if he were a very venerable and powerful patriarch, from whom the happy future had sprung. He had kept Rose, who represented the last generation in its flower, on his lap; and she had twined her arms about his neck, and was covering his face with kisses. His daughter Louise, his son Clément, had set themselves beside him with Joseph and Charlotte. And Sébastien and Sarah smiled at him and stretched out their clasped hands, while Thérèse and François, drawn nearer together, it seemed, by their affection for the august old man, seated themselves at his feet. At last Marc, deeply moved, almost stifled by the caresses heaped on him, said jestingly, with a pleasant laugh, 'My children, my children, you must not make a god of me! You know very well that the churches are being shut up.... I am only a hard worker who has finished his day. Besides, I don't want to triumph without my dear Geneviève beside me.'

He drew her near, taking her by the arm, and they all kissed her as they had kissed him, in such wise that the husband and wife, once parted, then reconciled and from that time commanding all possible happiness, were conjointly glorified in that elementary classroom, among those humble forms on which, again and again, the children's children, all the generations going towards the happy city, would take their seats.

And that was Marc's reward for all his years of courage and effort. He saw his work before him. Rome had lost the battle, France was saved from death, from the dust and ruin in which Catholic nations disappear, one after the other. She had been rid of the clerical faction which had chosen her territory as its battlefield, ravaging her fields, poisoning her people, striving to create darkness in order to dominate the world once more. She was no longer threatened with burial beneath the ashes of a dead religion; she had again become her own mistress; she could go forward to her destiny as a liberating and justice-dealing power. And if she had conquered it was solely by the means of that primary education which had extracted the humble, the lowly ones of her country districts, from the ignorance of slaves, from the deadly imbecility in which Roman Catholicism had maintained them for centuries. Some had dared to say, 'Happy the poor in spirit!' and from that mortal error had sprung the misery of two thousand years. The legend of the benefits of ignorance now appeared like a prolonged social crime.

Poverty, dirt, superstition, falsehood, tyranny, woman exploited and held in contempt, man stupefied and mastered, every physical and every moral ill, were the fruits of that ignorance which had been fostered intentionally, which had served as a system of state politics and religious police. Knowledge alone would slay mendacious dogmas, disperse those who traded and lived on them, and become the source of wealth, whether in respect to the harvests of the soil or the general florescence of the human mind. No! happiness had never had its abode in ignorance; it lay in knowledge, which will change the frightful field of material and moral wretchedness into a vast and fruitful expanse, whose wealth from year to year culture will increase tenfold.

Thus Marc, laden with years and glory, had enjoyed the great reward of living long enough to see his work's result. Justice resides in truth alone, and there is no happiness apart from justice. And after the creation of families, after the foundation of the cities of just work, the nation itself was constituted on the day when, by decreeing integral education for all its citizens, it showed itself capable of practising truth and equity.